THE BARROWS BELOW

Kelsey Elizabeth Nichols

ROISIN

The cold wind whipped around Roisin as she stood on the parapets watching the knights practice at arms in the courtyard below. Strong gusts blew her thick, black woollen cloak out behind her, along with her silvery, white hair. She welcomed the occasional chill to counteract its near excessive insulating effect. She would have welcomed a thinner cloak, but her Lord father insisted, lest she take ill and wind up like her Lady mother. As the heir to her house, that would behoove no one. So she wore the torturous thick cloak, and kept her complaints to herself. The black was her sole rebellion. The colour of her house was white, and at first her father had insisted on a white cloak to mark her as the future Lady and someone to whom was owed respect when she deigned to walk among the towns and the vineyards of her family's ancient holdings. She'd lied and claimed the white would be too arduous for the servants to launder, but in truth, she'd embraced the whispers of her being the "black hawk" of the family, and often thought that it suited her blue eyes better.

"My lady," a voice croaked from behind. Roisin turned around to behold the ancient castellan. He had been old even when Roisin had been a little girl, but these days he was positively decrepit. Not much hair remained to him, but the few alabaster white strands that did were impossible to contain, as though they were attracted to the creases of his impossibly folded and wrinkled skin. The castellan was half blind now, but remained in her family's service out of loyalty. Seeing blankly with his clouded eyes, he reached a trembling, bony hand out towards Roisin, searching for his Lady.

"Your Lord father," he struggled against the rushing winds, "has informed me that we have a visitor in the banquet hall and has requested that you attend them."

Roisin took his cold hand in hers, and began to direct the old man towards the door. "Thank you, Edwin," she said in a kind, comforting voice as she brought the old man back into the warm walls of the castle. "I shall go to him at once. Please, Edwin, spend the rest of your day in my library. It is warm there, and I do not wish for your bones to stiffen in this cold."

"But, my Lady," the old man began to protest, "my tasks for the day-"

Roisin hated to interrupt the old man, but if she didn't he was apt to go on all day and work until his legs gave out from under him. "I shall assign them to the stewards until after this storm has passed."

And with that, she took her leave before her castellan could protest further. Technically, she had no authority to order such a thing. That honour belonged to her Lady mother, but her mother was, well-

The castle of House Banfion was a labyrinth of towers and subterranean tunnels that seemed to stretch for miles and could easily confuse the uninitiated with perhaps fatal consequences. Legends claimed that the Banfion's had built their fortress atop the barrows and catacombs of the heathen kings of old. Roisin didn't know the truth of it for certain, but her personal adventures through the old, narrow tunnels that frightened the servants and made the elderly whisper didn't cause her to doubt the tales out of hand, either. The twists and turns of the tunnels, catacombs, and parapets were a meditative experience to Roisin, and she hardly noticed when she came out from behind a pillar into the main banquet hall of the castle.

Her father has seated at the high table, to the left of the seat reserved at the center for her mother, the Lady of the house. She noticed with a certain degree of glee the discomfort that such an arrangement brought to their visitors.

She knew why the party of four men were there, of course. Roisin had recently turned nineteen years old, and it was high past time that she choose a suitor and be wed. This of course hardly changed the fact that due to her circumstances, her pickings were likely to be slim until she came into her own as the Lady of House Banfion.

Their house was unique in the realm of Alderion, being the sole house to pass the title of its Lordship from mother to daughter. Other followers of the old ways prescribed their successors before the death of the current Lord, of course, or else hold a conclave to select the Lord after a death from among their number, but House Banfion stood alone in its strict matrilineality. It was not the oldest among the houses of the realm, having stood for nought but a mere one thousand years, but it had followed the will of its founding Lady, Awen of Lusca, to the letter ever since. That wasn't to say that doing so hadn't been enormously difficult. Were it not for the defensive position of their lands and their stranglehold on much of the economy of the realm, they were like to have been conquered many centuries ago. Their mode of succession was unpopular among the other Lords that kept to the old ways, let alone the other religious polities of the realm.

"My lords," Roisin announced from behind the gathered party, causing two of their number to visibly jump in surprise, "I apologize for keeping you waiting. I trust you have been provided with provision from our stores? The right of guests is kept in our House, and I wish to make you comfortable in our home at the earliest opportunity."

The leader of the party was an older man, close in age to her father. He was shorter than her father, portly, and greying at the temples but Roisin could tell from the finery that he'd arrayed himself in for this meeting and the erectness of his posture that he was a proud man, who wouldn't take well to what he may be perceive as obstinacy of her part. She decided to keep this in mind as she proceeded with their negotiations.

The man ignored her question, his first mistake, "When will the Lady of the house be joining us, since this man here," he motioned to her father with obvious contempt, "is seemingly not the Lord of his own table?"

He'd made his second mistake, but Roisin didn't let it show, "My Lord, as you're doubtless well aware, the Lady Eafyn has been ill these last five years, and will not be joining us. Instead, I will be entertaining you myself as the Lady Protector of Lusca, until such time as I come into the Ladyship in my own right."

The younger man of the party, presumably her potential suitor, made a passable attempt at a bow. "My Lady," he said, courteous where his keeper was not, "I'm pleased to make your acquaintance. We've been provided with the guest right, and I'd like to extend my thanks for your hospitality."

The short speech was clearly rehearsed, but it was better than nothing at all. The contempt to which some Houses held her own was always on her mind, and though she played the part of a high born Lady that was unbothered by such things, she had to admit that she was sensitive to them all the same.

"I don't believe we've had the pleasure of introductions," Roisin regarded the young man cooly. He was inoffensive to the eyes by any measure. He stood at least two heads taller than she did, and bore waist length, jet black hair that was tied and bound neatly at the back. He had dark, hazel eyes, a thin face, and a kind, sanguine countenance. He was comely, at the very least. Roisin noted that his surcoat bore the sigil on his house in bright blue thread – a seahorse beneath a shining north star. The Seastar's were an old Luscan family who had taken advantage of the astounding social mobility provided by the Old Way. Once a common fishing family, their contributions in trade and later their incredible ship building ability drove them from the depths of poverty, to landed gentry, and finally to the minor ranks of the aristocracy. Despite the old blood looking down on them, and the gods knew that Roisin could relate, their contributions to the Luscan naval forces and trade routes were indispensable. Hence why their current Lord dared to bring his son and heir to proposition her for marriage.

At her noting of their lack of introductions, he immediately sank down on one knee and gently kissed the sapphire ring that adorned her right hand. His father by rights ought to have performed the customary introductions, but Roisin appreciated the young man's initiative and degree of respect.

"Apologies, my Lady," he replied to her without a single hint of insincerity. "Allow me to introduce myself, I am Diarmid, son of Lukan, of House Seastar, and I am pleased to make your acquaintance."

Suppressing a smile and perhaps even a blush, Roisin motioned her hands and said "Rise, Sir,"

He did, and while still holding her hand and staring deep into her eyes, continued, "I'm here to ask before your Lady mother, who I am deeply sorry is too ill to be with us, and your Lord father that I may be able to court you, and may the Old Gods will it, eventually ask your hand in marriage."

Roisin suppressed a flush, making her countenance every inch that of an uncompromising, none too eager, and high born Lady of Lusca. She took a moment in a pregnant pause to choose her words with care, taking great pains not to reject the proposal outright as custom might dictate, while also maintaining and perhaps enhancing a fragile alliance between their houses.

She took a deep breath and began, "My Lord, I am most flattered by your proposal, and my heart sings at the thought of accepting it." His face and eyes lit up with a naive hope before she continued, "but I cannot accept out of hand. As you know, I will one day be the true Lady of Lusca, and my dear mother would be most bereaved from beyond her grave should I choose poorly in my husband. My spouse should add to the glory of this house, and to the renown of my future children."

Diarmid opened his mouth to speak, as though he thought that he ought to be partaking in ritual boasting to talk up his own claims, but Roisin raised her hand to signal that she wasn't yet finished.

"Buried deep within the barrow mounds of the Winter Queens of old, the progenitors of my house, the old Snowstone Amulet is thought to lie – a gift to Lady Awen from the great knight Eoghan before he set out on a suicide mission to slay the dragon Arosdiat, the black sky lord. He knew that he was going to his death, and laid powerful magic upon the stone – swearing to his fair lady that on another day, in another life, it would draw their souls together once again.

"I have had many suitors, Lord Seastar, but none who have truly desired my heart. Retrieve for me the amulet, and I will accept your proposal with joy and gladness."

Diarmid listened to her words carefully, before a genuine smile broke across his face. Clasping the pommel of his sword with one hand, and placing the other in a fist across his heart, he sank into a deep, and respectful bow. Rising again, he kissed her hand and said "To win the heart of Awen reborn, this is no task at all." before turning and leaving with his party to embark on his quest.

ELRIC

A gust of wind blew the flickering candle on the desk out, plunging Elric into blackness. He groaned in faint annoyance. The examinations were a mere three days away, and he didn't feel anywhere near as prepared as he ought to. He didn't care all that much personally, if forced to tell the truth about such things. That sentiment didn't apply to his Lord Grandfather, who not only expected but demanded exceptional results out of his sole male heir. The expectations of House Redwyn weighed heavy on his shoulders. He leaned back in his chair, the muscles in his shoulders suddenly screaming from the strain he'd failed to notice. A prolonged sigh escaped his lips as he leaned his head back and shut his eyes for a brief moment. It had been far too long since he'd welcomed the embrace of a good night's sleep.

A knock at the threshold of his study roused him from his plaintive rest. His eyes darted over to the entryway to the study, the gentle torchlight of the hallway cascading into the room and silhouetting the figure that had disturbed him. The lithe, weasel like form of Johanne, his steward, was immediately discernible to Elric. Rubbing his bleary eyes with his calloused hands, he yawned and asked "What is it?"

Johanne shuffled his way into the room, his skeletal like feet dragging across the floor as he moved. Elric had always assumed something had been wrong with him since birth, and took care not to point it out. The steward was like to have heard it all before anyways. The thin, younger man produced a folded parchment from his sleeve and handed it to the lordling. Elric inspected it, noting the grand seal of the Master of the Order adorned the yellowed paper intact.

"What's this?" Elric inquired as he broke the seal and strained to read the message against the faint light. After a pause, he handed the note back to his steward and rose. "Tell the Master I will be there within the hour. I need to freshen myself up before aiding in the admission of the new students – it wouldn't do for them to come under the tutelage of their future Lord in dusty robes."

Johanne bowed sharply and left as quickly and as quietly as he'd entered the room. Elric shut the door behind him and then pawed around on the desk for the match book. Striking it and re-igniting the candle, he carried the flame carefully around his quarters, from the study into his sleeping area. He tossed the old robes from his muscled frame to the floor, though his governess would have been loathe to see him do such a thing, he was sure, and acquired some fresh breeches, a vest, and a doublet bearing the sigil of his house on the left breast. He brushed his fingers across the embroidery. The black hawk bearing the rose of House Redwyn was enough to steel his resolves and provided respite to his weary spirit. He donned his clothing and made his way to the basin. The water was stagnant, having last been changed this morning or the night before – he'd been so engrossed in his studies that he couldn't quite remember, but it nonetheless felt cool and refreshing on his skin. He caught a look of his reflection in the unpolished mirror above the basin. His long, silvery white hair, ice blue eyes, and angular face stared back at him. He resembled the Heretics more than his Redwyn relations, so much so that his Lady Mother nearly drove herself to hysterics in her demands that he be named Eoghan before she passed. Instead, his Lord Grandfather decreed his name to be Elric, after the original true heir of Lusca.

He took a few more moments to gnaw on the stale bread leftover from whenever his rations had been served last. Sufficiently refreshed, he set off through the castle.

The Order of the Morning Star had been gifted the castle 500 years ago by the then High King of Alderion for the purposes of educating the youth of the realm in the sacred mysteries. While education was ostensibly provided through the mercies of the True Church and the Crown, as was on its face free to the public, in practice very few of the laity or the low born were ever given the chance to attend. Elaborate, floor to ceiling stained glass windows depicting scenes from the holy scriptures painted the hallways in rainbow colours that drew the mind to a sense of awe and wonder. Even after more than a year of attendance, it still had the capacity to take Elric's breath away at first glance – especially in comparison to his relatively dingy personal quarters. At times, the glamour and splendour of the place even dwarfed that of his home of Aylefield Castle, to say nothing of his true ancestral home of Saelmere – currently occupied by the heretic usurpers.

He put the thought out of his mind with a shake of his head as he neared the entryway where he was to meet the delegation of new students. The Master of the Order was already there, accompanied by Johanne. The slippery nature of his steward never ceased to amaze him, it was as if the man were made of smoke rather than flesh and blood. He approached, removing his black feathered hat from his head, placing it on his breast over his heart as he performed the customary bow and salute of the Order. It was only then that he looked up and took in the visage of the new students that he would be responsible for guiding and getting accustomed to the customs and dictates of the Order. There were three new students, two males and one female. They were younger than Elric by at least five years, and each one bore in their eyes a youthful apprehension and anxiety that he would do his best to alleviate by the end of this meeting. The two males were clearly brothers, both stocky with closely cropped black hair. The embroidery on their surcoats, a raised stag on a green etruscheon, signalled that they were from the Redwyn vassal house Latria. The young woman by contrast was conventionally pretty, and stood straighter than the two men, making her seem taller than the slouched, immature boys that she stood beside. The lowliness of her house, Salara, a line a mere forty years old created from its founder's bravery and service in battle to Elric's grandfather, gave away the reason immediately. The racing dogs of her house were nonetheless worn with pride. Elric smiled at her, and her cheeks flushed red. It was rare to see a female at the Order, especially one from such a relatively obscure and lowly house. Fathers who were adherents to the True Church rarely spared such an expense to provide such an education to their daughters, when sons were the ones who would succeed to their Lordship. He knew the Lord Salara had many sons indeed. He must have loved his daughter dearly, indeed.

The Master of the Order stopped the lecture he was giving on the illustrious history of the castle and the grand students who had studied within its walls when he at last took notice of Elric's arrival. He was an old man, downright ancient even. He was certainly older than Elric's grandfather at any rate. But, despite his advanced age, he carried with him the youthful exuberance of a green boy coupled with the strength of a mighty warrior half his age. Elric had personally watched the old man best even high born and well trained knights and lordlings on the practice fields. To say nothing whatsoever of the man's abilities with the Sacred Arts. The Master personified the phrase "Looks can be deceiving."

"Ah, there you are boy," he rasped at Elric, affection in his eyes for the young Lordling. "Children, may I present to you Elric Redwyn, heir apparent to the Lorship of Saelmere and of Aylefield, true Lord of Lusca and Aylemere, King of the Snowstone Mountains and the Sunset Islands beyond the Sea." Elric was surprised at the Master's use of his full title. While the Lords of Alderion were certainly permitted to retain their royal titles under fealty to their High King, they were not commonly used outside of official correspondence.

One of the young men perked up, a look of clear confusion on his face, "Lusca?" he asked, perplexed, "How is he the lord of Lusca? I thought the Redwyn's only held the forests of Aylemere. Isn't Lusca run by the Ban-"

Johanne cut the young man off, rage and indignation blaring through his voice in an uncharacteristic tenor for a man of such a slim frame. "How dare you imply that those wenches hold true in my Lord's ancestral home?! How stupid are you, boy? Who even let you in here with such a paltry knowledge of the Lord to whom your house holds allegiance!"

Elric raised his hand to silence Johanne as the Master angrily yanked the young steward back. "That's quite enough, Johanne," he said cooly. He turned then to address the young Latrian man who'd spoken up, "While it's true that the heathen women do occupy my ancestral home of Castle Saelmere, they are not it's rightful 'Lords'," he explained, with a somewhat mocking inflection on the word 'Lord'. "When my ancestor, Elric the Redwyn converted from the heathen ways of House Banfion to the true light of the Morning Star, he became, under the laws of much of Alderion, the rightful claimant to Lusca. Even under the laws of the Heathens, those women are unusual. May the Gods will it that they be rooted out within our lifetimes, and sanity be restored to that ancient realm."

Everyone present voiced their assent, and Elric began to speak once again, "Regardless of all that, your fathers have made a great expenditure to send you all here to receive an education, and, so I've been informed," he gestured to the Master, "learn the Sacred Arts. I've not been a student for very long, but if I may, allow me to demonstrate what you have to look forward to as a salve for those moments where you may find yourself in doubt of your purpose here."

Elric took several steps back, smirking with the full knowledge of why the Master had called him here over others. It wasn't due to any particular affection the Master held for Elric personally, though the depths of such were considerable in that regard. No, it had to do with the fact that despite his short tenure at the Order, Elric was something of a prodigy. A prime student to trot out for demonstrations of what any princeling could expect to learn at the Order, with a bonus side of propaganda that they may learn it quickly if only they came under the tutelage of the most experienced in the realm. It wasn't entirely true, of course. But it made for amazing recruitment.

Elric opened his palms and focused his icy eyes on them for a moment. He allowed his vision to unfocus slightly as he felt the power flow through him and the words he muttered from the texts of the ancient scriptures. All at once, his palms erupted into a glorious violet flame. It didn't burn or hurt, quite the contrary. It felt to him as though his hands had been submerged into a tranquil spring stream. That was the thing with magic, an opinion he held contrary to many of his colleagues at the Order and even to the Master himself. The dogma was that magic could come only from the taming of the forces of chaos through the use of the scriptures. That never worked very well for Elric. For him, true magic, true power, could only be found through the emotional depths and serenity within his heart. While it was unorthodox, the results spoke for themselves, he thought.

With a thought, the flames disappeared from his palms as quickly as they'd manifested in the first place. He reached his hand out and took the Salaran girl's hand, placing a gentle kiss on the back of it. He took a certain joy in her flustered reaction. "Come," he said to the students. "I'll show you the quarters where you'll begin your study of the old letters."

CIARAN

The young man took a healthy swig of his drink as he watched the scene playing out before him. The alcohol burned his throat but warmed his core and raised his spirits. He could scarcely believe what was playing out before his eyes, but he had to commend his sister's tremendous tactical acumen. It wasn't often that he got to watch a rejection happen in such a way that war was avoided. Still, he had to feel bad for the poor fool. No one had seen hide nor hair of the Snowstone Amulet in a thousand years, assuming that the glorified rock had ever existed at all. That wasn't to say the Ciaran didn't like the old stories. Quite the contrary, he loved them. But, he was a realist. He could recognize clever propaganda when he heard it, and the Gods only knew that his house needed as much of it as they could muster.

The fool made his exit, and his sister took a brief moment to share words with their father before striding in his general direction. He raised his horn to her in a toast and took another sip of his offensively strong drink before grimacing, and pointing out to his sister "There are easier ways to reject a man than a fools errand, sister."

Roisin furrowed her brow with a look of confusion and innocence that Ciaran knew in his core was fake. Ever the good actress, she was. "Whatever do you mean, Ciaran? I did no such thing. Once he retrieves the Snowstone Amulet, I will be happy to accept his proposal. The Seastar's are a fine, and noble family that we should be happy to enter into a closer alliance with. Perhaps you ought to lay off the drink, I fear it's affecting your senses."

Rage flashed behind Ciaran's dark eyes for a flash, but he swallowed it down with another sip of his drink. As much as he was loathe to participate in Roisin's games, he knew that his interference was generally unwarranted. Let her play, he would think to himself, it ultimately didn't concern him anyways. The fate of the Banfion man was that of the merchant, the castellan, or the warrior, after all. Petty politics ought not concern him as much as they did.

He sighed, "Good show then. I suppose his father can't make war on us for his son's own failures, after all."

Roisin took the horn from his hand, took a deep, impressive sip of his drink, and handed the horn back to him with an accompanying kiss of the cheek. "Now you understand," she smiled, "my dear elder brother. Walk with me, would you?" He did.

They made their ways through the halls of the castle, and it became apparent all too fast that they were making their way towards their Lady Mother's chambers. Ciaran was always loathe to see her in the state that she was in, especially after he'd been drinking. She wasn't conscious to judge him for it, of course. She hadn't been for years. That did little to assuage his guilt, and little to stop him from taking another sip as his sister opened her chamber door and beckoned for him to enter. The castle physician was there, as usual, taking her pulse and instructing her nurse in her tasks for the day. Yet, Ciaran somehow knew before any words were spoken that something was different today.

The doctor rose upon seeing his sister, and gave a deep, respectful bow, "My lady," he greeted her. Ciaran took another drink. He was well used to blending into the background at this point in his life. The physician rounded the bedside and took his sister's hand for a brief moment before allowing it to fall and proceeding into his report.

He lowered his head, his expression grave: "I'm afraid I don't have my usual report for you today. As you know, your lady mother's condition hasn't changed in some years, but I'm afraid that's no longer the case. The body can exist in such a simple state for some time, but not forever. Her heart has begun to fail. I'm truly, deeply sorry, my Lady, but we must begin to make the arrangements for our Lady's passing and your accession. I have informed your Lord Father already."

Ciaran heard a ringing in his ears as the physician spoke, barely taking in anything he was saying. He looked at his comatose mother, laying there in the same bed that she had for years now. He couldn't tell whether it was a trick of the light or if he'd really avoided seeing her for that long, but she looked thinner to him – greyer, and more sunken in on herself. He scarcely knew why it bothered him so much – functionally, his mother had been dead for some time now. Even still, he couldn't bear to be in the room any longer. He turned and left, ignoring his younger sister as she called after him.

Ciaran stormed through the halls of the castle, unsure of where exactly he was going. All he knew was that he just wanted to get as far away from that room, that husk that had once been his mother, as possible. He kept walking, faster and faster, near to breaking out into a run, before he turned a corner and ran head long into a figure less than half his height, knocking the five year old girl to the stone floors below. Her ruffled pink skirts dwarfed her unusually tiny frame. Ciaran instantly felt bad, and bent down to help his youngest sister up.

"I'm sorry, Shirra, I didn't see you there. Are you alright?"

The tiny lady rose to her feet, her eyes brimming with tears and her face crumpled with an expression of pain. His heart sank and then broke, just as the little princess of the castle began to wail uncontrollably. Ciaran pulled the little girl into a crushing embrace, "Shh, shh," he cooed, "Don't cry, sweet girl."

Shirra hicked and pulled away, wiping at her blighted eyes with still so small little fists. Her blonde hair, so much darker than his Lady sister's brilliant white, hung in tightly coiled ringlets framing her puffy, ruddy cheeks. Shirra was often neglected, and her heightened emotional states reflected that. In truth, she wasn't meant to be born in the first place. Their mother had suffered numerous miscarriages in the years after giving birth to his sister, so Shirra had come as something of a surprise. Their mother had scarcely recovered from childbirth before an incursion from the mountain clans called their Lady mother to the field.

She never recovered from her injuries.

Their father, on an emotional level, had always somewhat blamed the infirmity of his wife on his youngest daughter, though Ciaran knew in his heart that it wasn't on purpose. Shirra as such got more attention from her nannies and her governess than she did from her own family, and one only need spend five minutes with the little girl to know that she longed for nothing more than the gentle embrace of her family.

Ciaran took the little girl's hand, "Come on, let's go see our father."

Shirra's face lit up like full moon. She immediately stopped crying and joyously took her elder brother's hand before they set off through the castle.

In truth, Ciaran had bumped into his younger sister on the opposite end of the estate from their father's apartments, but he didn't think his little sister minded in the slightest. She seemed happy as a peach just to be spending time with her family for a change. They walked for close to an hour before finally reaching the threshold of their father's apartment. Ciaran took a deep breath, and then rapped at the door with several quick, authoritative, and successive knocks. A pregnant pause hung in the air, before his father's voice at last called out "Enter,"

Ciaran opened the heavy oak door and then crossed the threshold with with sister. His father, a bear of a man, sat hunched and shrunken over his large oak desk, staring half-heartedly at some papers. It was obvious from the glazed expression on his face that he wasn't really absorbing any of it. Ciaran presumed that he'd already heard the news from the castle physician. The man looked up at his son, and he seemed to Ciaran to be far older than his years. For the first time, the young man noticed the wisps of grey at his father's temples, and the etched lines around his eyes.

The man's eyes darted to Shirra, "What are you doing here, little one?" his voice was level, and not necessarily please. Shirra didn't notice. "Papa!" she cried as she broke from Ciaran's grasp and rushed towards her father, jumping up and into his arms. Despite himself, his father smiled for a brief moment and sat the girl down on his knee.

Ciaran decided to get straight to the point. Clearing his throat, he began, standing up straighter than usual: "Father," he said, "I think we could all agree that it would be good for me, and perhaps little Shirra here as well, if I started playing more of a role in the function of this house and family."

His father narrowed his eyes for a moment before quipping, in a good hearted way, "As what? The castle brewer?"

Ciaran took it in stride, even cracking a smirk of his own, "As enjoyable as that would be, perhaps not. I was hoping for you to assign me something, actually. Perhaps in the realm of our land's finances, or some building project? Something to keep me occupied and out of the castle for a time. I was thinking, also, that I could take little Shirra here along with me. Show her off to our people and give her something of an adventure."

Midir smiled at the thought, even as he stroked his youngest daughter's hair. "There is a task I meant to send you on, actually," the older man said in a pensive tone. "I was going to go myself, but I'm afraid that will be impossible now. I'll need you to attend the Grand Council of Merchants in Sasana in my place. It will be a three month long trip, and you will be leaving in three days. You have my permission to take your sister with you – she should learn how to be a proper lady and how to represent our house abroad."

Ciaran breathed in a sharp gasp, "Three months..." he repeated.

His father looked at him, his expression unreadable. "I understand it will be difficult for you. But, someone has to go on behalf of our house and our international interests. Your sister will be too busy with her accession, I'm sure, and I... I can't just leave her son. Not now, not at the very end."

Ciaran straightened up, still feeling the buzz from his prior session of drinking marred with a faint resentment. "If that's what's required of me, then there's nothing more to be said, is here?"

Midir shifted Shirra off his lap and motioned the little girl off towards her brother. "I'm sure she would forgive you, were she able."

Without another word, Ciaran lifted Shirra up into his arms and set off towards their quarters to pack. They were misfits, the both of them. Children who would never matter, nor be important. But, he could try his best, for both their sake.

And at least they were misfits together.

MAEVE

"Now is the perfect time for us to strike!" the woman seethed at her husband from across the table. The evening feast had been laid before them, and Maeve saw the moment as one that was as good as any to attempt to persuade her husband, yet again, on this matter. She was determined, despite the lowliness of her sex, to do her father proud.

Aengus, the Lord Lothric, glared at his wife in between bites of plump roast chicken. "Are you stupid, woman?" he asked pointedly. Maeve bristled at the insult. The Lord continued, "For the last damned time, I am not going to invade the territory held by my brother's spouse. By marriage, they are family and you would do well to remember the bonds of fellowship that such brings about between two warring Houses."

Maeve was undeterred. She raised her wine glass, the red liquid contained within it a jewel like contrast to her raven hair and alabaster skin. "Perhaps then your daughter will usurp your son. It would be good for our house to end their heresies once and for all. Otherwise, you might as well pass your crown to Maya." She gestured with her glass before taking a deep sip, enjoying both the fruits of her family's vineyards and the ire of her weak and ineffectual husband.

Aengus nodded and hung his head for a moment before saying, "You say 'our' house," he rose gradually, his eyes glaring daggers at his wife, "who's house do you mean? Ours, or the

Redwyn's?" he accused.

Maeve tensed up and pursed her lips, "Would helping your relatives by marriage not be aid to your own children? Should Niall one day require assistance, what better allies might be have than his maternal cousin when the boy comes into his own as the true Lord of Lusca?"

Aengus took a deep breath, composing himself before addressing his wife once more: "I will not have my house attack that of my brother to salve your old familial wounds, Maeve. While it is true that our children are cousins to the Lord Elric, they are also cousins to the Banfion children, my nieces and nephew whom I hold dear to my heart." Maeve opened her mouth to speak, but Aengus raised his hand to silence her before continuing: "I also frankly find it disgusting that you saw fit to raise this subject with me after we received the raven from my brother. Fool though he may be in not being the lord of his own manner, as my younger brother he had every right to marry for love under the laws of the Old Way. While I understand that you worship the Morning Star, I will not have this treasonous talk under my roof. Never raise this subject with me again."

Without another word, Aengus sat back down and resumed eating his, now admittedly chilled, dinner. Maeve scowled and asked, "Might I be excused, dear husband?"

Bored with it all, Aengus waved his hand to show his assent and continued to eat. Maeve wiped her hands on a kerchief, rose from the table, and walked off seething with her wine. She took off through the castle, much smaller than she was used to at her old home of Aylefield. Her Lord husband had never seen fit to expand the castle, even as their family and retinue grew over the years. While she respected his reasons as they related to maintaining the ancestral character of the fortress, even the most ardent historian would be hard pressed to not concede that the home often felt cramped, with little to no privacy. She made her way to the small study adjacent to her chambers, and bade her lady in waiting for prepare a fire and bring her appropriate writing materials. Maeve settled into her chair and small but ornate desk, wrapping some furs around her to guard against the typical Luscan chill as her lady in waiting rushed to make her Lady comfortable.

She was new, only having been in service to house Lothric for just under two moons. Maeve knew that she was a younger daughter of some hedge knight vassal of her Lord husband. In truth, she could scarce remember the girl's name. She was quiet as a church mouse and never made any requests of her at any rate. Regardless, she was a good and loyal servant. At the rate things were going, Maeve would be certain to set her up with a dowry large enough to allow her to marry well above the station in life to which she had been born. In due course, she got the fire roaring in the room's hearth and had delivered her lady's writing utensils before retreating to the halls after a brief curtsy.

Refilling her wine glass from the available bottle on the desk and after taking a deep sip, she settled herself and got to her work. She dipped her quill in the inkwell, the globs of black ink seemed to absorb the light of the fire from around it as she pressed the tip of the quill down on the page and began to write.

She wrote first to her father:

My Dear Lord Father,
I apologize for not writing you sooner. It has come to my attention that the invalid, usurper wife of my Lord husband's brother has reached her final extremity.

While I've done my best to convince the Lord Lothric to ready his forces for an invasion of Lusca before the usurpers can coronate a new wench from among themselves, if not for his own self respect but for the honour of his children and your dear grandchildren, I alas have availed naught. I know you will see this as a failure, Father, but I pray that it does not diminish any affections you may feel for me.

I shall continue to try and make my Lord husband see the light on the issue of the succession, but I fear that my influence within my own castle may be waning. I do not believe that our marriage has cemented the bonds of affection between our houses as you intended, and it pains my heart to come to this realization. I pray, Father, for whatever advice you may deign to grant me that I may better serve the interests of our fair and noble household.

I remain as always, you dear and faithful servant and beloved daughter.

Satisfied with her work, she fanned the paper briefly to dry the ink and prevent her handwriting for smudging. She then folded the paper crisply and applied the seal of House Redwyn to the page before leaning back in her seat in contemplation.

She'd never been all that close to her nephew, the heir to her house. The boy's mother died birthing him, and her brother had been slain on campaign very shortly afterwards. Her father had thus always been very protective of the boy, pulling out all the stops to educate him and bring him up to be a fine and worthy Lord of their house. Her father's lack of sons always troubled him deeply – it was all her ever talked about when Maeve was a little girl. He would regale her with the stories of all the great and noble men of their household. Eoghan the slayer of Arosdiat, Elric the Redwyn, Ailil the Proud – all spoken of with a holy reverence for their heroics. She didn't recall any similar stories about the Redwyn women. She smiled wistfully at the thought. Her only purpose was to be married off to an unappreciative Lord who didn't listen to her, her children summarily cut off from the greatness of their grand family lineage. At times, she even found herself envying the heretics she'd been raised to hate with every fiber of her being – though never for very long.

Maeve stared at the blank page, her mind racing with all the things she wanted to say to the boy but couldn't figure out how to word correctly. It had been years since she'd last seen him, and their meeting hadn't exactly ended on the best of terms. All the same, she knew she had to move now to help in securing his claim to Lusca at last. Despite her own personal feelings, despite her own sensations of abandonment, her loyalty to her house was absolute.

She picked up the quill and wrote:

Dearest Nephew,
While I am well aware it has been some years since we last spoke, I do hope that you have never doubted my deep and abiding affection for you, and my loyalty to you as the True Lord of Lusca and of Aylemere. I write to you now, my Lord and beloved nephew, to inform you that the time for your dear Lord Grandfather, my beloved Father, and by extension yourself to come into the fullness of your reign – the dream of your namesake, Elric the Redwyn fulfilled.

The matron of the heretics is at last in her final extremity. My brother by law reports that she's like to be dead within the fortnight – a failing heart from years spent in her bed. While of course the Lord of the Morning Star teaches us in the Holy Scriptures not to be glib at the suffering of others, and I imagine my nieces and nephews by law will be suffering terribly at this final loss of their mother, we must not allow this opportunity to pass us by like a ship in the night. We must work fast, dear nephew, to gather the support of other houses through which we share kinship and affinity towards the end of Elric the Redwyn's dreamed invasion to retake what is by rights our ancestral home.

To that end, I ask your permission that I might come to see you at the Order to discuss these plans which I have laid in person.

Your loving aunt and most faithful and devoted servant.

She read over her words with care as the ink dried to the page. Maeve could feel her blood pressure rise and her heart flutter in her chest. She sealed the letter with a sense of trepidation, unsure of whether her nephew was as like to read it or tear it into pieces and burn it in the hearth of his dormitory. All the same, she had hope in her heart that he would be able to put their differences aside, at least in as far as it got him closer to their family's centuries long held goal. With a careful hand, she addressed her letters and the summoned her lady in waiting.

"Yes my lady?" the diminutive girl asked in a voice as plain as she was.

Maeve pressed the letters into the girl's hand. "Take these to our rookery and have the master of birds send them out," she gestured to the letters individually, "this one is to go to my father at Castle Aylefield, and this one is to go to my nephew at the Order. No one is to break these seals nor be aware of these letters existence until such time as they are read by their intended recipients. Do you understand?"

The girl swallowed hard, clutching the letters in her hand tight. "I, I think so." the girl stammered. Maeve felt a twinge of remorse. She hadn't intended to intimidate the girl so much, but all the same she had to impress on the young lady the importance of secrecy in these matters. If the contents of her letters were read by unfriendly parties, it could very well spark a conflict that the Redwyn's would be incapable of winning on their own. The point was to bend the tides of war in their favour, not against it.

"Good," Maeve replied to the girl with a smile and a comforting pat of her hand. "Then run along. I'll make sure that you are well rewarded for your discretion."

DIARMID

The young man bore an enormous smile as he took his leave from the grand hall of Saelmere. The Seastar retinue followed close behind him, and though he could feel his father's glare boring into the back of his head, it did nothing to dampen his spirits. After all, how hard could the task set before him really be? He knew the Banfions to be honest and fair. Their Lady wouldn't send him to retrieve something that did not really exist.

When they'd made it some distance from Saelmere, Diarmid at last turned to Cian, his friend and squire. Cian was shorter than Diarmid, and of a more stout and stocky build. Despite his short stature though, the young man was a fearsome warrior. Diarmid once watched him crumple a knight's helm under his war hammer like a piece of wet paper. Even in light of his physical prowess though, it was perhaps the young man's mind that was all the more formidable. Cian placed a hand on Diarmid's shoulder,

"I know you've been given a boon, my friend, but are you sure this is a good idea? Surely there are other women out there who wouldn't put you to such trouble just to court them."

Diarmid gave his friend a sheepish smile, doing his best to remain stoic and suppress his true feelings. "That may be so," he said, "but they wouldn't be her."

In truth, Diarmid had admired Roisin for years. When he was still a green boy, his father sent him to train under the knights at

Saelmere. The training was valuable, to be sure, and it had made Diarmid into the competent knight that he had become, but it had never been the main thing he had focused on during his stay at the keep his his liege Lady.

No, it had been her beautiful heir. Day in, and day out, Diarmid would pray to all of the Old Gods that he might catch a glimpse of the fair, white haired, ethereal young woman. The grace and poise with which she carried herself spurred Diarmid on to improve himself – to be braver, more chivalrous, more learned with his blade and with his brains. All to make himself one day worthy of having a girl like Roisin to be his wife.

So while coming to Saelmere to proposition her had ostensibly been his Lord father's command, irrespective of what Diarmid himself might have wanted, it was difficult to suppress his glee at the idea. If he'd ever breathed a word of his infatuations to anyone, it might well have been different, he supposed. But, perhaps not. After all, the Banfions were the Ladies of Lusca, to which his house owed its very existence. To have even the chance to join them together in matrimony and raise their own prestige in so doing was something that Diarmid was all to sure his father would strangle an infant to achieve.

In time, they found their horses and Diarmid was content to let his father take up the point with all his pomp and nouveau riche circumstance. Lord Lukan was a proud man, in a manner he didn't often deserve. He would bark orders at the servants in a scant imitation of the grace and dignity of the older houses to which they owed allegiance, to say nothing of the Banfions, would make simple requests. Diarmid often found himself cringing at his father's behavior our of an innate sense of decency, and endeavoured to treat their retinue better when he had the power to do so. As a result, dangerous murmurings of a coup from among his father's sworn swords reached his ears more often than he was comfortable with. Diarmid had urged his father's councillors and knights to stand down on more occasions than he'd ever admitted to Cian, let alone the man himself.

Diarmid rode in silence, preferring the simple company of his friend and his mare, a beauty as black as the summer's night sky, to idle conversation. After a few hours of riding, they came at last upon the town of Vasser where they were to rest their horses and spend the night. It was three days of riding between Saelmere and the Seastar coast where their keep stood. The cold made his father miserable, but Diarmid revelled in it. Fat snowflakes caught the light in a string of rainbow pearl like sunlight, bringing a glamour and glory to the Snowstone Wood that evoked images of the great Fey Kings and Queens from when the world was young. He found himself so distracted by the beauty around him that Cian had to call his name more than once, lest he ride his horse dead long into an oncoming tree.

The town of Vasser was a quiet hamlet, but looks could be deceiving, as they so often were in Lusca. What seemed peaceful on its surface hid what were perhaps some of the best blacksmiths and armourers in Lusca, and perhaps all of Alderion proper. The sun was setting as they gave the reins of their horses to the stable boy of the town's inn. Diarmid caught himself in another brief moment of romantic wonder lust, but he shook it aside. He had work to do.

A young maid, clearly under the tutelage of the ancient and rotund mistress of the inn, greeted their party at the door. She gave a deep, perhaps inappropriately so, curtsy – first to Lord Lukan, and then an even deeper one to Diarmid that she followed up with a smile that made her seem all the more younger than her years. "Might I take your cloaks and see to your needs, my Lords?" she offered to them.

"Yes, yes, on with it." Lukan said dismissively, tossing his cloak in the general direction of the young maid who caught it with deft and astute hands. Diarmid and Cian removed their own outer garments, passing them to the girl with gentleness before taking their seats by the roaring hearth. Diarmid rubbed his hands and faced his palms towards the flame, wishing that that chill didn't so easily permeate his leather gloves when he rode for extended periods.

In time, the mistress of the inn came round with a heaping, piping hot pot of the establishment's signature stew. She and the maid set rustic, carved wooden bowls before the party before serving them stew, bread, and ale in their order of precedence – a ritual that the patrons of the establishment were well accustomed to. Lukan complained about the minutiae, as usual, but the women took it in stride. In truth, they were used to the Lord's vociferous tantrums and complaints. They often didn't amount to much more than a poor tip at their worst.

Cian and Diarmid dug into their meal, the hot broth which warmed the young men's cores was complimented nicely by the cool, refreshing taste of the ale – the mistress's own brew. Diarmid felt the warmth from the alcohol and the stew spreading from his core out to his near frozen extremities, and despite the negativity of his father, he felt content.

The mistress and the maid came round once again to refill their bowls and tankards, remaining blessedly quiet as the party ate and drank. When Diarmid at last felt sufficiently refreshed, he turned to his still feasting friend and said:

"You and I need to formulate some sort of plan. This thing ought not to be difficult, but we shouldn't attack things like a couple of green boys either, don't you think?"

Cian replied with his mouth partially full, "You and I?" he teased his childhood friend.

Diarmid pushed his friend on the shoulder with a playful grin,

"Yes, you and I," he chortled, "who else would be stupid enough to go with me into some creepy old barrows to retrieve a gemstone?"

"Who else would be foolhardy enough to propose to the heiress of Lusca?" Cian retorted.

Diarmid played into things, as he always did, "Exactly. Now, you know other bone headed idiots just like the two of us. Who might have the honour of your recommendation for joining this merry little search party of ours?"

Cian grinned at his friend, "Devon, Geoff, and Tuirean might be bribed into such a foolhardy endeavour with enough promised ale, I suppose."

They were lowly hedge knights, all of them, but Diarmid knew them to be reliable and merry young men, the sort that oft found themselves champing at the bit for their chance at adventure and glory. In most respects but for rank, which in truth Diarmid himself had yet to earn in his own eyes, they were one and the same. Though with any luck, that would be different after earning their fame through the retrieval of the Snowstone Amulet. Diarmid had sworn to himself that he would remember his friends and anyone who had aided him when one day he found himself raised to his father's noble rank in the peerage. Judging by his father's failure to amend his attitudes towards others, he supposed that day wasn't far off in coming.

Diarmid shook off his momentary sense of gloom and sought instead to focus on his own future. The affections that he felt for Roisin were no doubt genuine in nature, having lasted as long as they had. His heart was aflutter at the very thought of being able to spend any amount of time with her, let alone at being granted the honour of asking for her hand in marriage.

The conversation at the table grew to a rowdy roar as the

knights and retainers drank themselves into a joyful state of inebriation. A companion of his father placed his hand on the grouchy man's shoulder,

"Come on Lukan, sing us that song! The one you wrote about your wife's sister before you decided who to bed and wed!" The man's words were slurred from the alcohol, as were those of his father through his vain protests. Diarmid couldn't help but to smile. His father was a gleeful drunk, at least. He'd been told by some of his father's men that when he drank with them, he became once again the hopeful and kindhearted young man from their youth. It was his sudden ascension to the Lordship, they'd told him, that had changed his personality to one so diametrically opposed to the man they knew. Stress, they told him, with a gloom filled tone that seemed to imply that Diarmid would be like to meet the same fate as his father.

As he watched his father at last acquiesce and break out into a bawdy tune with the friends of his youth, Diarmid couldn't help but despise the fatalism common to men who kept the Old Way. One's fate was for sure spun by the goddesses at one's conception, but the old priests, the ones that were sometimes called heretical, had an antecedent to that foundational belief of the Old Faith – if one sought to impress the gods through their might, cunning, or valor, their fate might be changed to one more favourable and pleasing to them.

Even if Diarmid had been fated to become a disagreeable, vociferous, and haughty minor noble, he was determined through his own deeds and prowess to be the one to change that. He would win battles, he would philosophize and inspire men to follow him, he would raise their lowly house scarce worthy of note to a major player in Lusca and all of Alderion besides.

And most importantly, he would enter the barrows, retrieve the Snowstone Amulet lost long ago, and marry the glorious young woman of his dreams that so many would have considered too far above his station in life to even dream about. Each man was better than his birth, said the old maxim, and Diarmid was determined to see that it was true.

ROISIN

Grey eyes opened, and for the first time in five years seemed to behold their dear husband and the unknown young woman beside him, bearing hair so white it seemed silver as the moon and blue eyes so like those that had once been her own. A rasp of air escaped her lips, as though she wanted to speak but had long since lost the power. The woman, far aged beyond her years, closed her eyes. And at last Eafyn, Lady of Lusca and Queen of the Snowstone Mountains and Sunset Isles beyond the Sea, was dead.

Roisin blinked as she felt the life go out of her mother's flesh. She didn't know what to feel. For the most part, she just felt numb. Placing her mother's lifeless hand over her still heart, she rose to her feet, quelling a slight tremor with her free hand. The castle physician sank into a deep, reverential bow "Your grace," he addressed her. Roisin froze with the realization, and without another word left the room, everyone present, including her father, rising and reverencing her as she made her exit.

The next two weeks went by in a blur. The castle physician took Lady Eafyn's body to the coldest portion of the crypts in order to preserve it long enough for extended family members to make their way to Saelmere in time for the cremation and accession ceremonies. Roisin found herself uncharacteristically avoiding the tunnels and crypts. Even though she was unlikely to come across her mother's corpse, the idea of her being down there at all gave Roisin feelings of intense discomfort. She didn't know why. On any functional level, her mother had been dead for years after all. She moved about the keep in something of a haze, preferring to distract herself with the immediacy of her work. Even in the absence of ceremony, she became the Lady of Lusca at the moment her mother's heart ceased to beat, and the tasks required of her office never seemed to cease, not for a moment. While she had performed many of these tasks anyways, her Lord father was no longer eligible to act as a regent alongside her. For the first time in her life, Roisin felt well and truly alone – the black hawk staring down from her high mountain roost indeed.

At last, the day of the cremation and her accession came. Custom dictated that the old Lord must see the accession of the new, and so Lady Eafyn had lain in the crypt until this day. Roisin spent the morning greeting her guests, taking their condolences and their congratulations, not terrible interested in any of it. It was a day that she had once dreamed of, the day upon which she would wear her mother's ancestral crown, clothed in silver and glory, despite her better nature. Now that it was here, it just felt empty.

All at once, Roisin was all but dragged away from the Lords she had been exchanging pleasantries with by her ladies in waiting to get ready for the ceremony. By the time they'd made it to her chambers, the ones that years ago had belonged to her mother and were the largest in the castle, a warm bath had already been drawn for her. Roisin didn't protest. She removed her clothing and got into the bath, trying her best to tune out the drone of her maids readying her dress and the gentle pulls against her white hair as they washed and braided it for her. The hot water bore a stark contrast to the chill outside, and felt good against her skin. They directed her to rise from the bath and began to dress her in a fine, white and silver gown. It had been decided, that at least for today, it might be best if the Black Hawk of Saelmere dispense with her funerary garments and port something better able to inspire hope and awe in her new subjects. Metal adorned the garment, tradition among the Luscans, and the ladies then bejewelled her, hair, wrists, neck, ears and all in drooping sapphires. When they were finished, they brought a mirror to Roisin that she might approve of their work.

At first, Roisin didn't recognize herself. The woman staring back at her from the mirror looked more akin to the Fey Queens of legend than her own countenance. Her blue eyes and rare hair, combined with the gleam of the jewels and the metal gave her something of an otherworldly appearance. She wondered for a moment what the distant memory of her mother would have thought.

It came time to make their way to the place of ceremony. Roisin walked first through the halls of Saelmere, the change in the order of precedence not lost on her at the slightest. The air in the halls felt thick and in a way enigmatic, as though all the past Ladies of this great keep were watching her in a cautious judgment, unsure of whether she would carry on their legacy of glory or damn their line to a finality of conquest. Roisin did not sense her mother among them.

They soon exited the castle and walked some feet to the Banfion ancestral Stone of Destiny. A great oak tree stood above it, and the priest waited below it with the sacrificial horse and the throne of Lusca. The horse bore hair as white as her own, and the tree was bare but for a few remaining blood red leaves. The priest was an old man, staring at her with a blank expression upon which Roisin might have projected anything. Her retinue came to a sudden stop at the edge of a stone circle, allowing Roisin to approach the priest, and by extension the gods, alone.

"Who comes to make treaty with the gods for the ancestral throne of this land?"

Roisin stretched out her hand, beckoning for the priest to take it as she genuflected first towards the oak and then to the stone. "I have come," she gave the appropriate response, having practiced the rite for a week without ceasing. It made for a good distraction from things.

The priest took her hand, laying a gentle kiss upon the dorsal side of her hand to demonstrate his symbolic approval of her rule. He then produced a sapphire ring adorned in silver dragon wings from his sleeve and placed it upon her finger.

"With this ring be you wedded to your realm," he said. Roisin voiced her assent, then rose at the priests invitation. He broke first into a long sermon, exhorting Roisin to rule justly, with grace and with kindness, and a remembrance of Awen and the Fey Kings and Queens of old. She was to take the advice of her councillors were it was warranted, but to always remember that she ought to make her decisions and take due responsibility for them. It all felt a little generic, as though the priest had given this same speech dozens of times, only sprinkling in her name on occasion in a vain attempt at personalization.

Soon however, they came to the main event. The priest and Roisin together invoked the gods and goddesses, all her ancestors, and the ancient spirits of the land of Lusca – with the priest providing the customary calls and Roisin the responses. In time, the gathered assembly beyond the standing stones began to chant, at which time the priest provided Roisin with a sickle, razor sharp and ready for the task at hand. Singing the ancient songs, Roisin seemed to float towards the horse, stroking its silver mane gingerly with a hand that looked all the more alabaster against the gloom of the skies and the white of the snow. Whispering an ancient prayer, she closed her eyes then brought the sharp of the sickle across the animal's throat in one swift, clean motion. The animal didn't even see the blade, and let out nary a whimper as it's life's blood poured fourth from its wound like a waterfall. Roisin felt fast to the animal as it collapsed, doing her best to help it go down with grace and gentleness. She whispered the soothing prayers into its ear as she felt the life go out of the mare. It felt nothing like the death of her mother. Somehow, despite the inherent violence of the act, she felt that the animal felt peace in its heart as it passed from this life into its next. The priest caught the blood within an ornately carved wooden bowl, proceeding then to pour half of it down a hole at the base of the tree, and reserving the other half. He dipped a branch of mistletoe within the pool of blood which he held, and sprinkled it upon Roisin.

"Take this," he intoned, "the blessing of the Gods and Goddesses, that you may reign well and long."

He set down the blood and produced from a hidden hollow in the tree the ancestral crown of Lusca – silver oak branches adorned with dripping sapphires. Roisin sat upon the throne, and was thus crowed:

"I crown thee Roisin, daughter of Eafyn, Lady of Lusca and Queen of the Snowstone Mountains and the Sunset Isles beyond the Sea. May you be a Queen of Elfhame and of man upon this earth."

The crowd intoned their assent, and then together, Roisin and the priest partook in sprinkling the blessed blood upon those present. Her mother, placed outside the assembly, was the last to be sprinkled before Roisin put her to the flame.

The festivities of the evening were both joyous and immensely draining to Roisin. Her family and all of her Lords who had gathered to watch her accession made merry under the light of the moon and candles. Yet, on some level, she couldn't help but wonder if what they were really celebrating was the fact that they now had a living Lady rather than anything about her personally. She wondered if they were really celebrating the end of their realm's long nightmare of being headed by an invalid – if they were really celebrating the death of her mother.

At some time past midnight, well towards three in the

morning, Roisin felt an inexplicable pull towards the crypts. There was no need for her to go down there; her duty to lay her mothers ashes next to the other matriarchs of her household lay three days away. And besides, the festivities were no where near over. Yet, she felt the pull to go down into that morbid earth all the same. With the cat like sleuth she still possessed, perhaps she remained the Black Hawk after all, even after all the magic, pomp, and ceremony, she slipped away unnoticed from the celebration and into one of those dark tunnels that she knew all too well.

She wandered into those catacombs without the aid of a torch, relying wholly on her memory of the meandering paths and narrow archways. The oppressive atmosphere that had kept her out of this place for the past two weeks seemed to have dissipated. Instead, the air felt oddly light. Roisin let the darkness comfort her, unsure of where she was going. It was then, that she saw it.

She blinked at first, unsure of whether or not her eyes were playing tricks on her. A faint blue glow emanated from the end of the hall. Roisin quickened her pace, a faint feeling of apprehension mixed with an odd peace formed in her heart as she sped towards the source. The light grew brighter as she made her approach, until finally, she saw.

At first glance, she could have sworn it was a shade of her ancestors. Until she looked closer. The white haired woman was tall, much taller than any woman she'd ever seen. Her features were extremely angled, and her wholly blue eyes slightly too large to be human. Faint drops of white sat where the pupil ought to have been, assuming Roisin's eyes weren't playing tricks on her in light of the gloom and the sapphire glow.

"Roisin," she intoned with an unnatural timbre that resembled that of a bell, "at last, I find one with the sight."

ELRIC

"Sir," Johanne knocked on the door and then entered the room, "I brought your supper."

Elric rubbed his eyes, exhaustion over taking him. The meagre fare of the Order was most welcome after the horrific day he'd had. "Thank you, Johanne," he gave a tired, sheepish smile, "Please place it on the table. You may go."

Johanne looked crestfallen, "Are you sure, sir? Perhaps you'd benefit from someone to discuss your findings with?"

Despite himself, but probably due to fatigue, Elric snapped in annoyance. "No, Johanne! Now, leave the food and go!"

The servant did as his master bid, and Elric began angrily eating his stew. The past several weeks had been nigh on unbearable for him, between his studies, acclimating the new students under his charge, and of course, the news from his aunt. To say that he felt troubled would be an understatement. The Latrian boys were a lost cause, he'd decided, only there to enhance the prestige of House Latria through the barest associations with the order. They possessed no aptitude for magic whatsoever, and struggled to read the simplest of sacred texts and Old Letters, let alone comprehend them in any meaningful way. Attempting to mentor them had been an exercise in frustration for Elric, sending him to the confessional on more than one occasion for his sin of internal wrath. The Salaran girl, her name was Yenn, as Elric had bothered to learn, showed more promise. She understood the texts readily, and asked questions so thoughtful that occasionally Elric had to stop the lessen prematurely and look up an answer for her. She'd even begun to sense her inner mana ahead of schedule. She impressed him.

Of course, his studies and the news from his aunt worried him more than his students did. He kept finding references in the Old Letters that gave him pause, and the Master's schedule and his own never seemed to line up in such a way as to have a meaningful conversation about his concerns. There had to be a rational answer, of course. The Order had been around for thousands of years, surely someone had asked the very same questions Elric had before during the vast expanse of the centuries.

With a heavy sigh, he pulled the offending page out from the mountainous pile that threatened to topple over everything else Elric stored on his cell's desk. His brow furrowed as he read through the words in Eldar. He had to be mistranslating the words into common speech, he thought. After all, there was only one high god.

Wasn't there?

He surveyed the paper again, taking care to read the words on the page carefully and with intentionality. The language was definitely slightly beyond him, but he could think of no other conclusion for the words he was reading – over and over again, they seemed to indicate the existence of an entity that pre-dated the Morning Star. In frustration, he whipped the offending paper across his cell's table and rose from his seat, rubbing his aching temples. He flung his cloak around his shoulders, feeling comforted by the fur lining, and set out from his quarters. Perhaps a walk and a trip to the library would ease his concerns.

The air outside of his cell felt lighter than it had within, even though the hallways were dramatically colder than the personal rooms of the students and order members. Winter was coming on strong in the southern regions of Alderion, and far sooner than anyone would like. Elric pulled his cloak closer to his body and picked up a brisker pace. As he strode through the halls of the ancient castle, several individuals stopped to bow and curtsy towards him, mostly vassals of his grandfather, but not all. Heartening as it was to see the support of houses who owed his no loyalty, he didn't have time to return their affections.

The walk seemed longer than it usually did. Of course, Elric knew the reason why. He normally had friends or retainers to keep him company, and no journey was ever long if punctuated with pleasant conversation. Keeping his head down, he broke into a light jog towards his destination, desperate to drown out the deafening silence.

He burst through the doors of the library, drawing some attention and the inevitable shush from the patrons within. The ambient sounds of the roaring, comforting fire and the din of flipping pages brought Elric's heart rate down, however. He moved towards one of the many hearths in the warm room, rubbing his hands together and allowing them to absorb the ambient heat. His eyes darted to the person sitting in the large, luxurious arm chair by the fire. It was a younger man, younger even then the Latrian boys. His surcoat bore the northern star, identifying him as a vassal house to his own, though one so minor that Elric struggled to remember their name. When the younger man realized who was standing before him, he immediately rose to his feet, placed his right hand over his heart, and sank into a bow so deep and relevant that it brought a twinge of embarrassment to Elric's heart.

"My lord," he gasped, clearly starstruck, "Forgive me, I didn't realize that you'd entered the library. Here, take my seat by the fire, it's ever so cold out!" he rushed, near falling over himself, to one side, offering the chair to Elric.

"That won't be necessary, truly," Elric smiled, motioning with his right hand for the young man to resume his place. "In truth, I need to peruse the library for some important papers and will be far too busy talking to the librarian to enjoy this marvellous spot you've found for yourself. Please, resume your seat. Take no more trouble on my account."

The young man protested, but Elric didn't stay to hear it. He turned and left the fireplace, making his way towards the upper levels of the library. The ancient oaken steps creaked under the slightest pressure, and added to the ambient but quiet din of the library as Elric moved. The institution, like so many other things in the Order, was divided by rank. Recent inductees like the young man below were limited only to the ground level. Neophytes on the other hand had access to floors two through four. Acolytes like Elric has access up to the sixth floor. Only true masters of the Order had access to the papers and effects held on the forbidden seventh flood. Few ever reached that level. The rank of acolyte was enough for most houses – after all, no other school in Alderion could provide an education such that the Order was capable of. Still, his curiosity sometimes got the best of him. Even though he doubted he would ever be inducted into the illustrious ranks of the masters, after all, he had little aspiration to be a cleric, the knowledge that they held was tantalizing to him. A forbidden fruit that made him salivate at the thought.

The shelves made for a confusing maze, but eventually Elric located a librarian on the fifth level who might be able to help him. She was old, but not quite as old as the Master of the order. Her face was slightly lined, but in the right lighting still retained the dying embers of youthful vigour. In her prime, she must have been quite the striking beauty indeed. She held her head high and proud, as befitted a lady of noble blood. Elric came through at her periphery, giving the customary bow of the order in a sign of greeting and respect.

The librarian nodded, returning his respect, and said in a voice far more youthful than her visage might otherwise suggest, "How can I help you, young man?"

Elric rose from his bow. "I had some questions for you, my Lady, if you don't mind assisting a lowly acolyte with his studies of the Old Letters."

The librarian studied him cooly, noting the sigil of House Redwyn on his surcoat, "Are you not under the direct tutelage of the Master himself? Why don't you ask him instead?"

Turning on his charms, Elric replied, "Alas my Lady, I've tried my best in that regard. But you know as well as I do that he's a busy man. He hasn't the time to help me with such things. In fact, I think he wants me to seek out the answer on my own. But, there are seven levels to the Order's grand library, representing the seven days of creation. And I am ill-equipped indeed when it comes to searching through such a vast cornucopia of knowledge on my own. So I come before you, on bended knee if I must, to implore that you assist me."

The librarian smiled at him. "No need for that, young man." She placed the book she was holding on the shelf. "I can make time for a dedicated student. Now, what is it that you're having difficulty with? I can direct you to the right place."

Elric grounded himself before continuing, "Well, you see, I was tasked by the Master of the Order to study the Old Letters, as you know. And I fear I may have missed one of my lessons in Eldar, as I seem to be reading things that contradict the sacred scriptures."

The librarian grabbed Elric by the arm and pulled him in between two rows of shelves. "Not so loud!" she hissed at him between her teeth. Staring daggers at him with her eyes, she grasped his shoulders tightly, her fingernails digging in to his flesh through his cloak and surcoat. Elric winced. Her anger gave off an aura of fury.

"Who gave you those papers?"

Elric tried to pull away, "No one," he said before correcting himself, well aware of what a grave sin it was to lie to a superior in the Order, "Well, I don't know. Not really. They came with the rest of the papers I was supposed to study. I don't know who puts my packet together, a lower servant I suppose."

The librarian seemed to calm somewhat, releasing her grip on Elric and adopting a more composed and kind expression. "Tell me what they said, or what you remember of them. In as much detail as you can."

Feeling a twinge of anxiety and guilt, like a child caught red handed in the baker's lauder, Elric began to elucidate what he'd read. "I know my Eldar isn't the best, and I intend to go to the confessional for my sin of inattention," he began.

"That is not issue," the librarian motioned for him to continue.

"They seemed normal at first, going on about the sixth level mysteries and how we apply the old incantations in Eldar to our magic, how they enhance and add power to that which is latent in the student. But they began to mention other entities that I haven't learned anything about yet. I'm aware of the existence of the angelic forces, and if that were all it was, I wouldn't ask."

The librarian stared at him. Elric couldn't read her expression.

"They seemed to imply," Elric was choosing his words with care, unsure by the librarian's expression of how she would react to what he had to say next, "the existence of a God above the Morning Star. But that's not possible, is it?"

The librarian smiled sweetly at him, and replied in a tone even more honeyed still, "Of course not, my boy. I will need you to bring those papers to me immediately though, so I might investigate who tried to fool you with such blatant lies. Can you do that for me?"

CIARAN

The gentle spray of the ocean waves was refreshing to Ciaran as he watched his father's men load his and Shirra's belongings on to the ship. It was a large and impressive galley, as would befit the siblings of the High and Noble Lady of Lusca. Ciaran bristled at the thought. On some level, he understood why the other men of the realm reacted so strongly to the succession strategy of his house. The thought came to him often, of course, even though his loyalty to his family was absolute.

He stared at his younger sister, the now heir presumptive to the throne of Lusca. Shirra had been given a new cloak by their sister, lined in the silken soft fur of the mountain great wolf and embellished in hawk feathers and sapphires to reflect her new status. Ciaran found it a bit ostentatious, but he couldn't help but smile at the simple joy Shirra got out of "playing princess". They wouldn't be there for the accession ceremony, of course. But in a way, Ciaran thought it was better that way. Shirra hardly understood her place in the world as it was. She didn't need to be further confused by the expectation of mourning a woman she never really knew. It was better for him, too. As much as he was loathe to admit it, he was better used towards a purposeful end rather than sitting around the castle, drinking, and wallowing in his self pity.

Their belongings successfully loaded onto the ship, the captain came to collect Ciaran and Shirra. "My Lord," he addressed Ciaran, using his courtesy title in a reverential rather than mocking tone, "your cabin is ready for yourself and the Lady. Might you accompany me on board? We will be disembarking shortly."

Ciaran nodded and shouted for Shirra, who bounded towards him with the happy exuberance of childhood. The young girl had scarce ever left Saelmere in her short life, let alone the land of Alderion entirely.

Ciaran bent down to her level, bringing the little girl into an embrace. "Are you ready?" he smiled at her.

"Yes!" she replied, practically jumping for joy.

"Then let's get going!" Ciaran scooped her up into his arms and followed the captain up the gangway. The sailors aboard shouted bawdy taunts at one other as they prepared to un-moor their vessel for the open waters. Ciaran placed his sister on his shoulders and made his way to the bow of the ship, standing at the rail to watch the galley lurch forward into the water. Their movement started off slow and then picked up speed as they advanced from shallow to deep waters. The spray of the ocean splashed up into their faces, and while Ciaran grimaced, Shirra giggled hysterically at the joy of it all.

Before they knew it, they were off – sailing from the continent of Alderion west towatds the islands of Sasana. While Alderion had some warmer areas, sometimes bordering on subtropical in nature at its southernmost reaches, it was by and large a cold place. The islands of Sasana, on the other hand, were a veritable paradise upon their world. The weather was consistently warm, bordering on outright sweltering, for the whole year round. Ciaran half remembered the reason behind it, something about the water current carrying warm air from the planet's deserted equatorial regions through a unique confluence that centered upon the archipelago. It mattered not to Ciaran. While the islands of Sasana were a center of commerce and finance, he felt that the people who lived there were perhaps a bit too pampered by the warm weather they were blessed by. When Ciaran was a boy, a young man from Sasana came to stay at Saelmere for a time to learn from their merchants. Ciaran found him to be insufferable, constantly complaining about the cold and the apparent scarcity and poor quality of the food provided to him.

No matter, he thought. He would spend his time there as his father instructed, make good for the interests of House Banfion and the Luscan region at large, and then go home. If he could make the experience a positive one for his sister, all the better.

The sun was going down fast now, and Ciaran looked up at his sister. "What do you say we retire to our cabin and get nice and warmed up?"

The young lass was shivering, though she was trying her best not to let it show. "Yes," she said meekly. Ciaran took her off his shoulders, set her down, and took the little girl by the hand.

Their cabin was easy enough to find. His father had chosen a trusted captain, who often ferried lesser Lords and Ladies to Sasana and other mercantile continents. It was located right next to the Captain's quarters, and was significantly larger besides. They entered through the ornate door to the blessed warm room – one of the ship mates had already kindled their fire for them. Shirra removed her cloak and ran over to the hearth, rubbing and warming her cold little hands by the warmth of the fire. Ciaran called out for a ship mate, assuming one was nearby to hear him.

Of course, the response was near immediate – Ciaran suspected that due to the nature of the ship, they had some men routinely assigned to the duty of caring for the Lords and Ladies whom they ferried along with their goods. He was around Ciaran's age, but rough looking from the lifestyle that he lived. He stood about a head shorter than Ciaran, pointing to some form of malnutrition in his childhood. The young man had the wiry but lean look that indicated muscle growth through use and punishment rather than the extensive training at arms that Ciaran had undergone. Disshelved brown hair partially covered his striking blue eyes, and the stubble that adorned his face could have one easily mistake him for a man older still.

"Yes m'lord?" he replied to his superior in the more informal register of the common man. Standing at attention, he awaited Ciaran's response.

"Thank you for starting our fire," Ciaran began, "but it seems that you forgot to set our table for supper. What's on the menu, my man?"

The young man adopted a look of fear and anxiety. Evidently, he was not yet accustomed to the duties of his station, but was all the more used to suffering the consequences from cantankerous noblemen. While Ciaran did have high expectations, he wasn't much in the mood to abuse the young man.

Though he was a bit impatient at the man's silence: "Well, what is it?" he pressed.

"W-w-w-whiskey stew," the man spat out at last, his anxiety clearly overwhelming him.

"Excellent!" Ciaran's eyes lit up, "Now, there is a way to make me happier still, my man. Do you know what it is?"

The ship mate shook his head, though he seemed to be put somewhat at ease. "No," he said with an almost exaggerated degree of caution, "how can I do that?"

Ciaran smiled at him, "If you tell me there's still whiskey left over to drink, and provide me with as much as you can spare over our journey."

The younger man smirked at him, "Sir, this is a trading ship."

Ciaran laughed, "Good man."

The man took his leave and in time came back with all that Ciaran had requested, along with a bag of sweets of Shirra – who tore into them greedily. The man set the table, and portioned out the food. Ciaran sat, inviting Shirra to abandon her sweets and sit like a proper lady as well. The man turned to leave, but Ciaran felt compelled,

"Stay," he extolled, "eat with us."

"Oh, I really couldn't possibly," the young man replied.

"Nonsense. Your duty is to attend the Lords that you ferry, no? As you can see, my travelling companion is but five years of age, and I desire intelligent conversation." Ciaran tore a piece from the bread at the center of the table, pointing at the empty chair across from him. "Now, sit."

The man did, portioning himself some food and drink.
Ciaran took dipped his bread into his stew and took a chunk out of it. Still chewing, he asked, "What's your name?"

"Wilem," the man replied, sipping his whiskey. He made something of a face at the bite of the alcohol.

"You must be new," Ciaran chuckled, taking an unhealthy swig of his own drink with a straight face. "Come on, take it like a man."

Willem took another sip, and more successfully reduced his pained expression at the burn.

Ciaran smiled, deciding not to torture the ship man any further. "So, Willem," he started taking bites of his stew. It was alright, but nothing to write home about in comparison to the lauders of Saelmere castle, "Where are you from?"

"The Seastar coast," Willem replied, "Technically, anyways. I grew up there, but my mother was a member of the Snowstone mountain clans."

"A mountain man?" Ciaran breathed, unsure if he was impressed or on some level worried.

"Half of one anyways," Willem replied, chewing the meat from his stew. "My mother was a war bride. My father was just a pike man during one of the skirmishes. He killed twenty mountain men single handedly though, and for that Lord Lukan honoured him with a knighthood. Well, after he captured my mother, anyways."

"Normally, it's the other way around," Ciaran observed, "The mountain clans marrying civilized women through the right of capture."
"It is," Willem agreed, "but under normal circumstances, it wouldn't be something we recognize in Lusca, no?"

Ciaran nodded.

"Unless it's a Luscan man capturing a mountain woman."

He nodded again.

Willem shrugged, "Laws aside, most people on the Seastar coast, apart from Lord Lukan anyways, considered me a bastard. No one would squire me, at any rate. Even if I did come from a more conventional pairing, most people view the mountain blood as a taint – don't think I didn't see the way you looked at me. It's alright, I'm well used to it." Willem gave a rueful smile.

Ciaran looked at him pensively, "And what about the mountain clans, how do they feel about you?"

Willem gestured at the air, "They'd accept me well enough, I suppose. So long as I proved myself in battle."

"So what made you want to be a ship hand then?" Ciaran inquired, "Why not make the Seastar coast accept you? Or just go off to the mountains?"

"That's the thing," Willem took a far deeper drink, his skin flushing with the warmth of the liquor, "I don't really know what I want to do. Sometimes I want to be a knight like my father, win glory on the field and maybe raise our family's station in life. But then I remember that my mother was a warrior in her own right, gods I miss her, and there's no reason why I couldn't rejoin her family if I really wanted. I don't know. I suppose growing up by the sea, it called to me. Maybe if I travel the world long enough, I'll have some kind of epiphany, figure out who it is that I really want to be.

Ciaran listened with care, and chewed his food in silence for a few moments. "You know," he finally broke the pause, "I understand."

Willem looked confused, "How? You grew up in a ruling family. You can do anything you want to."

"That's the thing," Ciaran smiled, with a slight slur as the familiar comfort of drunkenness washed over him, "I can't just do whatever I want, nor can I follow the path set out for me as it exists either."

Before Willem could respond, the Captain called out for him and entered the room.

"Are you drunk?!" he shouted at his private.

Ciaran waved him off, "At my insistence, my Lord. Pay him no ill will." He rose from his seat and produced his purse from his trunk, handing over a fistful of golden coins to the Captain. "This should more than cover the time I intend to take from you, my Lord. I'd like Willem here to sup with me nightly, or as often as I may require."

In truth, the money Ciaran had given him was many times the price of their own passage, bordering on double the profits the captain could have expected to receive from the voyage. He bowed to Ciaran: "Whatever you need, my Lord. We are always happy to be of service to House Banfion."

MAEVE

"My Lords," Maeve gave a deep curtsy at the gathered assembly in her main hall. "I thank you for taking the time to travel here to Lusca today. I'm aware that the weather has been most disagreeable, as of late."

Lord Althorp grunted then huffed, "It's no matter, my Lady," he said in the gravely tone he'd grown famous for. He was an aging man, nearing his mid sixties, and always bore a hacking cough that announced his presence long before he entered a room – to say nothing of his size. In spite on the shrinkage of age, he was still a bear of a man – standing at six and a half feet tall, with the girth of a brick wall. Suffice it to say, his household tailor was paid most handsomely indeed. Yet despite it all, Maeve could tell that he was not a well man. His cough, when it was not an incessant bark, sounded wet and melancholic. Often, the man gasped for air between fits. Maeve had even heard rumours of a bloody handkerchiefs being hidden by his loyal courtiers.

She eyed the man's wife. To say that Lady Althorp was far younger than her Lord husband was an understatement. The young woman was less than a third of her husband's age, and his fourth wife in as many decades. At the least, it seemed to Maeve that he'd married this one out of a sense of genuine love and affection. She was an Alderion Rose, to be sure, tall and fair with the ruddied cheeks of a youth in love, her vitality undimmed by the stresses of child rearing and political machinations. Yet all the same, her mother had been a minor Banfion, which made her one as well despite all the nominal laws of the realm. Maeve could use this.

Lord Althorp broke into another fit, and his Lady immediately tended to him, "No my love, no," she cooed, turning to her superior Lady. She curtsied deeply to Maeve, and while still in a deep bow, entreated the High and Noble Lady:

"My Lord husband is too humble, my Lady," she kept her head bowed – it was clear that her Banfion mother had drilled the intricacies of precedence into her daughter from a young age. She continued,

"But as you can see, my Lady, he is not a well man, and I fear that despite the splendour and grandeur of your hall, he might be a bit too cold."

Maeve smiled at her, showing no visible offence, despite her irritation at a woman so young daring to tell her anything. "Of course my Lady, how thoughtless of me." She gestured for the hand of Lord Althorp, "Come, my Lord, we will go further into the interior of my keep. Where it's warm. I'm sure Lord Aengus will be most gladdened by your company."

The Lord gratefully took Maeve's hand, and shambled up the steps with her. The rest of the retinue followed behind them, taking their places in the unspoken order of precedence. The Lord Starkfall who had just come in to his keep brought up the rear, whereas the Lady Merwyn, an elderly crone who seemed twice the age of Lord Althorp, took up the middle with her head held high in the style befitting that of a woman of an ancient and proud house.

The fires in the interior had been allowed to burn low in the lady's absence. The servants were not expecting their lady to return so abruptly, and the panic was stricken upon their faces as they scrambled to warm the rooms and make provision for their distinguished guests. Once the room was warm and food provided, Maeve invited everyone assembled to take a seat.

"Where is your Lord husband?" Lady Merwyn croaked.

"He'll be along in due coarse," Maeve assured the elder woman, taking her hand in her own, "He's inspecting the Lothric men at arms at present, surely you must understand."

Lady Merwyn assented, and all assembled dug into their food. Eating and drinking first before getting to any important business was a custom in Lusca, and one which all assembled were well acquainted with.

At halfway through the meal, Maeve set down her platter and broke the silence. "My Lords, my Lady," she addressed her guests, who also stopped eating in quite as much earnest. Custom ran deep in Lusca. "I suppose at this point you'd like to know why I've gathered you here today. I'm aware that my letters were most terse, but you must understand that things are being put into motion which cannot get to the wrong ears."

Lord Starkfall spoke next, out of turn but Maeve forgave it. He was young yet, and essential to her machinations.

"Well, I question whether there's a rest stop between now and the point, but I suppose you'll tell us in your own time." He paused for a moment before quickly adding "My Lady."

Maeve gave him a terse smile. "Well, let's dispense with the formalities then, I'm certain that a young Lordling such as yourself has many important matters to attend to." She folded her hands in her lap. "As you are well aware, the Usurper Lady Eafyn has finally succumbed to her injuries. Her bastard daughter," she noticed Lady Althorp stiffen. She softened her tone. "Her daughter has assumed, falsely, the throne of Lusca. Now, as you know, my Lords, I am most devoted to my husband, the true born Lord

Lothric. But I fear for the safety of this realm, and all the realms of Lusca, if this succession is allowed to stand."

Lord Althorp coughed mightily before asking gruffly, "You are a Redwyn, are you not?"

"I am," Maeve confirmed, anticipating the question to come next, "You are wondering what this has to do with you, I wager?"

The elder man nodded.

"My Lord, you have four daughters, and to my knowledge your young wife here has recently given you a son. This young false Queen, this Roisin, she's known to be a great beauty indeed, and somewhat conniving. Should she come to greater prominence, well," she motioned to his wife, "who is to say that any future daughters given to you wouldn't succeed him in your stead, granting the lands which your father's have held in trust by the Gods for thousands of years to a usurper from within? Should we allow the Banfion's to regain their old standing in this realm, you may well lose all that which you've been granted by divine providence. Your line brought to a most abrupt end, indeed."

Lord Althorp looked incensed, but guffawed, "That will not happen." Maeve eyed his young, pretty wife. She refused to meet her gaze.

Maeve turned to Lady Merwyn. "You were born a Redwyn, aunt to my dear father, and great aunt to myself. Your grandaughter is wife to our current High King. You hold great influence in our courts."

Lord Starkfall interjected, "And your designs for me?"

"Cousin," Maeve smiled, "It's well known that your men at arms are some of the most well equipped from the sands of Asyut to the Sunset Islands and beyond. To say nothing of your own prowess in battle. I've heard the tales, and in fact I've begged my own Lord husband to hire you on retainer to train our own Knights. Only the best will do for our household, I think, and you are nothing if not the best."

Maeve was nothing if not an expert in laying flattery on thick when it mattered. Thus disarmed, Lord Starkfall looked more amenable to what she had to say next:

"I propose the following. We fulfill the dreams of our various ancestors, and that of the great Black Hawk, the Lord Elric of old. You, Lord Althorp, are one of the richest men in Alderion besides the Banfion's themselves. Your sway with the merchants of Sasana is second only to our High King himself, besides the stranglehold those women maintain. I propose that you use this power. If we can take advantage of this young Roisin's weakness and naievitie, we can wrest their mercantile power away from them. Cut the purse strings, and the loyalty of their vassals will most certainly follow."

She turned to the Lady Merwyn, "My Lady, you are one of the most respected and powerful women in the realm, and you have my deepest condolences for the passing of your dear husband. But I would ask that you not shut yourself away in your widowhood as you have. You still hold great sway in this realm, greater than I fear you have been willing to wield until this moment. I would ask that you write your dear grand daughter, and have her take the ear of our High King. The Banfion women are the only ones that have been suffered to succeed one other as they have. There must be something within the laws of the old believers or that of the Church of the Morning Star that would at last bring an end to this centuries long string of usurpation and abuse. Use your voice my lady, I beg you, and at last bring sanity and godliness back to these kingdoms."

Lady Merwyn nodded. Nothing more needed to be said on her account. She was a woman on few words, but what ones she had were nothing short of a bond held in blood.

She turned at last to Lord Starkfall, "When all this has been accomplished, my Lord, I would ask for your assistance. My nephew, Elric, is the future Lord of Aylemere and the true Lord of Lusca after the death of my dear father, which I fear will come sooner than any of us may be able to bear. He is young yet, my Lord, younger than you are now. And he will need your help to take that which is his birth right. I know you are a believer in prophecy, my Lord, despite our differences in religion, which while I find unfortunate need not divide us as kinsmen. Is it nor fortuitous that the current heir to the Black Hawk be named for the first who took up the mantle to assert his rights and that which he believed to be the will of the divine? Help him to take that which is his, my Lord. And I would further ask this of you," she paused.

"What, my Lady?" Lord Starkfall looked at her plaintive.

"That you befriend him, my Lord. Teach him how to be a man worthy of that which I would have him take. Oh, the Master of the Order does his best, but he cannot replace the guiding hand of a father, nor can he provide the fraternal affections of an elder brother. Elric was the only child of my late brother, and I thank the light of the Morning Star that he has survived to adulthood. But he cannot rule without guidance, and I fear he is not ready."

"I can try, my Lady." Lord Starkfall assented.

Maeve clapped her hands together in joy, "I am so glad we could all come to an understanding. Now," she motioned for the servants to bring in more food and drink, "Let us eat and make merry in celebration of the accords which we have come to, and the glorious future that we might create."

DIARMID

Diarmid woke with a pounding headache and the remnants of a dull roar between his ears. He stared at the ceiling, trying in vain to make the wooden boards above him stop spinning. The evidence of the prior night's debauchery was all around him. The fire burned low in its hearth, letting a dull chill into the room that permeated Diarmid's bones and made his feelings of malaise all the more intense. Groaning, he rose from his bed and surveyed his surroundings. Cian was splayed across the floor in front of the dwindling fire, snoring with the beginnings of two black eyes forming on his face. That ought to please him, Diarmid thought as he snuck past his unconscious friend to feed more logs into the fire. It soon came back to life, bringing warmth with it against the oppressive cold. His head spun, even as the fire made him feel marginally better. His eyes scanned the room.

Geoff, Tuirean, and Devon were all passed out at the inn table across from the bed. Presumably as the son of their liege lord, they allowed Diarmid to take the bed when they had all decided at last to call it a night. He didn't recall asking for it, but he knew that these friends of his would have insisted, despite or perhaps even because of his protestations. Bottles and tankards of ale and whiskey littered every available surface in the room. Someone had carefully stacked several of them a top the sleeping form of Geoff – it was obvious now that he had been the first to pass out. Several off the bottles were half empty – in their drunken haze, they hadn't even bothered to check on their original drink before cracking open another.

Diarmid found an unopened bottle of mead and cracked it open, taking a healthy swig of the honeyed liquid. Almost instantly, his sense of impending doom and the feeling that his limbs were made of solid lead began to abate. He grabbed some now stale bread from the table and began to chew on it. This also made him feel better.

He wracked his brain to remember what happened the night before. Cian and himself had arrived on the Seastar coast early in the day. It didn't take them long at all to locate the men they had decided should join their merry band of fools. They had all been located exactly where Cian had expected them to be: Geoff in the inn, harassing the local cheese monger for a chance at an apprenticeship, Devon brawling in the inn, and Tuirean training with his Lord father's blacksmith. Some said that Tuirean's friendship with the Lord's son and heir was the reason for such a lofty position, but in truth that wasn't the reason at all. His friend simply had a passion for molten metal and iron things. In fact, the friendship had been the reason it had taken so long for the blacksmith to take him in, much to Tuirean's nigh on infinite frustration.

Cian and Diarmid went to each location in turn. Diarmid gave his spiel to each friend, talking at length about how useful marrying the Lady of Lusca would be for their town, but even more so about his own personal love for her. He was sure he sounded something like a tottering fool, with the comparison between the young lovers and Eoghan and Awen of old being a trite and tired stereotype. Nonetheless, his friends grew excited. Whether it was out of a wish for his happiness or the chance at personal glory, it didn't matter. They were on board with his foolish plans, and that was all that mattered.

Of course, the schemes of young men were nothing if they weren't backed up with merry making and celebration. Devon suggested that they seal their arrangements with a round of libations at the local inn, and things escalated from there. One round turned into two, then two into three, and by that point the young men were loud, boisterous, and banished from the lower hall to the rooms above where their celebrations grew all the more out of control. The night turned into a blur of singing, dancing, drinking, eating, and even a friendly brawl between friends. Despite the fact that Diarmid was paying a mighty price for it now, he couldn't help but smile. Times like this were good, and he was all too aware that the good things in life were fleeting – to be savoured while they lasted, and looked upon fondly in one's later years.

He heard a groan from the floor, and readied himself with some food and drink for Cian. His friend took refreshment from him greedily. "Do I even want to ask what happened last night?"

Diarmid chuckled, "You could, but I wouldn't be of much help. I scarce remember it myself."

"Then I assume we had a good time,"

"We did," he held his hand out for Cian, helping the man to his feet. "But we should start planning how we're going to do this. We've burned enough daylight as it is."

Cian nodded and set to rousing their other friends. Diarmid made his exit and headed to the bathhouse. This inn was unique, and perhaps premier, among others in Alderion for its habit of keeping the baths warm at all times. Keeping the fires beneath them ever burning was an expensive and time consuming process. It was simply too much effort for most inns, who preferred to focus this efforts on keeping their guests plied with a constant supply of warm food and cold drink. At times he wondered how their revenues justified the expense, but whatever their reasons, Diarmid was glad of their practice. He removed his clothing, placing them in the receptacle provided to be laundered by the staff, and readied himself to enter the water. A clicking sound behind the wall indicated to him that his old clothes had been taken, and new ones provided in their stead. Being a future Lord had its perks, he supposed, as he lowered his aching body into the warm water. Calming steam rose around him, and he near dozed off into sleep.

A knock at the door roused him. "Diarmid?" Geoff called out. "They served us out a meal for before we leave. It's uh- getting cold."

Diarmid called out his agreement to his friend, rose, dried, and dressed. In a few moments, he was back in the room he'd shared with his friends the night before, now noticeably cleaner, to break his fast with them in a better way. The bacon, soup, and bread were all piping hot and fresh. The salt made him feel all the more right as rain.

In time though, with the food and the drink all cleared from their sight, the full weight of what they were setting out to do came down upon them. No one had seen hide nor hair of the Snowstone amulet in 1000 years, what chance did they really have of finding it? In silence, the group bade their farewell to the inn staff, with Diarmid paying them most handsomely indeed. As always, the inn keeper greeted him warmly and with the respect due to the son of his liege lord. The stable boy was waiting for them outside, dutifully leading them to their well rested and prepared horses. Diarmid took note of the fact that they had even gone to the effort of pre-loading their bags and provisions onto the animals' saddles. Donning his cloak and checking the security of his sword, Diarmid gave a few extra gold coins to the boy, and mounted his horse, prompting the others to do the same.

His horse had in fact been his own. The beautiful mare had been with him for some years now, and Diarmid felt in tune with her essence. She had even ridden into battle with him on more than one occasion. Her black hair was silken and smooth beneath his touch as he gave her a gentle pat of the head before taking the reins and setting their group forward.

The day was bright and far warmer than it had been the day Diarmid set forth from Saelmere castle. The light bounced off the melting icicles and snow, which still retained the rainbow beauty it held before – albeit in a different way.

They rode for some time in silence, before Cian took the initiative of riding up beside his friend.

"Is something on your mind?" he asked, taking note of his Lord's anxious expression.

Diarmid was silent for several more minutes, lost in his own trains of thought that refused to release him to a coherent response. His friend, concerned, called out to him again,

"Diarmid?" he asked, the concern in his voice growing all the more urgent.

"Hm?" Diarmid's head shot in the direction of the noise. He blinked several times, his brain struggling to comprehend and interpret what he'd heard. At last, he responded, "Yeah, I suppose there is. There isn't much to be done for it though."

"Did you want to talk about it?"

He didn't, not really, but the road ahead of them was long and cold. Silence would not make the time or the miles pass any faster, but talking might bring a welcome distraction.

"The Saelmere barrows are thought to be cursed," he said in a low voice, "have you ever heard the story?"

"No, I haven't."

With no better options, Diarmid decided to tell it, "It's thought that the spirit of Arosdiat haunts the deepest recesses of the barrows. He was so angry to be slain by Eoghan that he swore never to allow his spirit to reunite with the Lady Awen. The story goes that anyone who tries to retrieve the amulet, lest they truly be Eoghan himself reborn, will meet with a terrible death in the jaws of the dragon's shade."

Cian's guffaws were so loud that they broke a nearby icicle off of it's feeble branch. "That's so ridiculous!"

Diarmid stared at him from astride his horse, "You think so?"

"Course I do!" Cian was laughing so hard that tears pricked in his eyes. He wiped them away, wincing with slight pain from the extra cold the moisture brought with it. "Haunted barrows are one thing. Everyone's barrows are thought to be haunted. It's the realm of the dead, after all. But don't you see that story for what it is?" he asked, trying his best to calm the chortles that still shook his bear like frame.

Diarmid narrowed his eyes. Cian was ever the skeptic. It was one of the few traits of his friend that annoyed him to no end. "I'm not sure I follow."

"It's just an anti grave robbing story!" Cian exclaimed. "It's a story that the Banfion's especially tell so that no one will be stupid enough to rush into their barrows and steal something valuable. Even though they cremate, they still bury their urns with considerable riches and jewelry. It would be a pay day for anyone to just go in and take everything. So, they simply made up the story of Arosdiat. Even the Grand Master of the Morning Star would think twice about rushing into a Banfion grave if it bore with it even the slightest possibility of having to fight a dragon, let alone that one."

Diarmid didn't agree, of course, but he nodded and kept his thoughts to himself for now. While Cian wasn't necessarily a non-believer, he tended towards that instinct sometimes more often than Diarmid was comfortable with. He looked at the horizon. They still had plenty of light, but that would fade fast during the height of a Luscan winter, he knew. He brought his mare to a stop and dismounted with a hand gesture to his friends:

"We can go no further today. Everyone dismount, we'll make camp here. It will be two more days of riding until we reach the barrows. I'll take first watch, and we leave at dawn."

ROISIN

"My lady?" Roisin heard the knock at her chamber door. She elected to ignore it, but it came yet again,

"My lady, please, there are important matters that must be attended to." Edwin's voice cracked from behind the door. Intense feelings of guilt shot through Roisin as she rose, dressed, and opened the door. Her nights had been much more like early mornings as of late, and the demands placed upon her during her daylight hours were beginning to become overwhelming. Yet all the same, it ought to be worth it in the end, she reasoned. The knowledge she was on the cusp of elucidating in her tired mind was intoxicating just to think about.

"Come in," she called out. The door opened at a glacial pace. It was becoming all too clear that the elder man would soon be no longer capable of performing his duties, and yet he persisted. Out of love, loyalty, or a simple refusal to die, Roisin didn't know, yet she admired it all the same.

The old man trotted into her chambers. "M-my lady," he bent into a bow. The creaking of his bones as he did so made Roisin wince. Roisin took the elder's hand, allowing him to place a gentle kiss upon her ring. He straightened his posture, his old bones creaking even more audibly. Roisin tried not to let her discomfort with the sound show, lest she shame him inadvertently.

"Lord Lukan's delegation is in the main hall, my Lady. They

wish to discuss the spring trade cycle with you."

There was nothing that Roisin wanted to do less, but she nodded in acquiescence all the same. Lord Lukan had been relentless since Diarmid had left on his quest, and it was beginning to wear on Roisin's patience. The constant reminders of the Lord's wealth and strategic importance made her resent Diarmid by association, though he'd done nothing to deserve the sentiment. Sighing, she patted the folds of her gown and took the arm of the elder. She developed a newfound gratitude for Edwin's shuffling pace. The longer she spent roaming the halls, the less time she would have to spend entertaining sailors who she knew all too well would rather be at the tavern house themselves.

Roisin took a deep breath before entering her hall. Where before she had no qualms at all about acting as the regent of her realm, now that she was such in her own right, tiny doubts had begun to sink in. Before, she need only act in what she believed to be the best interest of herself or her realm. After all, she had been nothing more than a dutiful daughter acting in the name of her invalid mother. Now that all eyes were on her, with no one to reflect on any poor decisions before she could make them, the pressure was beginning to wear her thin.

"My lords!" she addressed with a glee that no one but herself knew was fake. "Such a pleasure to see you here in my halls. Might you partake of all the hospitality that Saelmere has to offer."

The men rose at her approach, holding their hats in their hands with their heads placed into a slight, respectful bow, an address befitting that of their liege Lady. They only took their seats once again when Roisin sat upon the high hair and motioned for them to do so. With a gesture, provisions of salted meat and wine were brought before the men, and Roisin implored them to eat and drink their fill. At around the halfway mark, they got to discussing the business of the day proper. It was nothing of note, at the end of the day. It was the same as it had ever been, simple notes and permissions granted for the same sea routes the Seastars had always taken. She found herself wondering why she didn't simply delegate the task, though she knew in her heart that the personal presence of the Lady of her House was a necessity if the loyalty of her vassals was to be assured.

The business concluded, Roisin rose and excused herself, bidding the men to continue partaking of her hospitality. She was sure they would be more than happy to oblige – the appetites of sailors were most voracious indeed. She made her way through the castle, hers now, in every sense of the world, still unused to the deference she was given by all those whom she passed. Never again would she have to curtsy to anyone, except perhaps the High King of Alderion himself. It was an arresting idea.

Confident that no one was watching, she slipped into a hard to see alcove in the wall – one of many throughout the castle, that led down into the tunnels and crypts below Saelmere. It was here that she had forged her connection to her blood, and it was here that she would continue to train until it came time for her to venture deep into the Snowstone forests to cement her claims.

She wandered the tunnels for what seemed like an hour until her intuition told her that now was the time to stop. Lowering herself to the ground, Roisin sat in a prayerful position on her knees for a moment, allowing the coolness of the earth to penetrate through the folds of her gown and to the bones of her knees. Closing her eyes, she placed both hands down upon the earth and breathed in deep. Once her mind felt clear, it became trivial to sense the currents of energy flowing through the earth beneath her and the air around her. The world seemed almost electric. It was enough to send her senses into a near swoon. How she hadn't been exposed to this part of reality before now beggared belief. After all, if the faery woman was to be believed...

She stopped, the thought bringing her back to a new found focus. The words of the ancient tongue escaped her lips exactly as she'd been taught, and the air around her burst into a flurry of blue flame. Despite the dance and burn of the fire, it felt as cold as ice against her flesh.

The presence at last returned. "You are doing well," it intoned from behind her in a soothing, matronly tone.

"I wouldn't be here without your guidance," she replied, her gaze lowered in a most humble fashion. "Why was I never taught any of this before?"

"Our power resides within your blood, but not all those with the blood of Awen may connect with the ways of old."

"I – I don't understand." Roisin stammered, the flame flickering for a moment with the quivers of her uncertainty. The presence reminded her to maintain her focus, and the magic flowing through the air stabilized in short order.

It continued: "It is not necessary for you to understand. Simply reach through the secrets of the Blood."

"How?" Roisin asked.

The presence put its cool hands upon her shoulders. "Close your eyes," it intoned, "and feel through the Blood as you feel the earth, and the water, and the life force of the Great Goddess all around you."

Roisin did as she was bid, and the great blue fire grew stronger around her. The presence made sounds of approval, and then instructed her further "Now reach through the Blood, through the past, and call forth that which you see."

Roisin was beginning to know better than to ask for an explanation. This was not the magic of the Order; this was primal and taught through feeling and action rather than through long winded explanations or the lectures of wizened old men. Clearing her mind, she attempted to do as the presence instructed. At first, nothing of substance seemed to happen. The odd colour flashed across the vision behind her eyes, but nothing more than that. She began to grow frustrated at herself, and her seeming inability to figure out the art based on instinct alone.

"Patience," the presence told her.

Roisin took another deep breath and cleared her mind once more. Then, it happened.

Grey mists opened up before her, the vista of a sea blanketed in the fog of an early morning. The oceanic view seemed to spread out for an eternity before her, and with that expansion she felt her own spirit picking up speed. Her presence moved slowly at first, but then began to speed up exponentially until she was flying across misty waters at a blinding, inconceivable pace.

And then, she saw it. A swift sunrise and white shores. Standing upon the high white cliffs, they were there. The shades of Queens and Kings long past, high born and noble Lords all. She knew on an intuitive level that each and every one of them had some grand achievement and legacy to their name – names which reverberated and carried their inexorable power throughout history.

For what seemed like an eternity, they stared at one other – the spirits of the thousands long dead boring the pressure of their expectations through Roisin's heart. The weight of it was enough to make her feel as though she would buckle beneath it. Yet she held firm. In the back of her mind, she knew that she was the result of all of them, the culmination of all they had achieved throughout their lives.

She reached out a spoke a word. In an instant, she snapped back into her physical form with a force that knocked her backwards. Flat on her back, she stared upwards at the roof of the cave, her world spinning. She sat up. The blue fire and the presence were still there, but now there was something more.

A grey vortex, reminiscent of the waters, swirled before Roisin's eyes. She looked to the presence, and it nodded. Reaching out with her left hand, she grasped it. It felt viscous and cool beneath her fingers, and yet still too ethereal to be a solid. She spoke the word again, in a tongue more ancient than even that which covered the walls in the oldest portions of the crypts. The vortex contracted and then exploded outwards in a brilliant flash of white flame. In its wake, they stood.

Shades of long dead warriors, armed and ready for battle. But they were not the regular knights and men at arms she was used to.

They were beautiful. Their tall, slender frames topped with hair white as her own, and eyes that shone with a sapphire brilliance. The females bore ethereal wings in hues of blue, green, and violet, while the males towered over even the largest of her knights and struck fear into her heart with their black, feathered wings. Their weapons looked to be made of an icy metal, with cruel serrations even with their gilded embellishments. The figures were transparent, but she knew that they were real all the same. In some ways, they were even realer than the presence itself.

The tallest of the warriors, the one Roisin presumed to be the leader, walked towards her before drawing its sword and getting down on to one knee in an expression of fealty and loyalty as old as Lusca itself.

"Do you accept them?" the presence asked of her. It dawned on Roisin then that she indeed had a choice to make. Thinking back at the Queens and Kings of old she saw standing along the shore though, she knew in her heart that the decision was made before it had even been presented.

"I am Roisin, daughter of Eafyn, of the House of Banfion. True born descendant of Awen, Lady and Queen of Lusca, the Snowstone Mountains, and the Sunset Isles beyond the Seas. I demand your loyalty as you would have given to Awen herself, and I ask that you fight for me. What say you?"

In response, the remaining warriors all drew their swords and knelt before her. Then they disappeared into the mists from whence they came.

ELRIC

Elric couldn't help but to yawn. The Priest's sermon had gone on for two hours now, and he had yet to learn anything useful from it. He'd come to the Priest with that intention, to be sure. But, there was only so much repetition of the basics of the Order's theology that one could reasonably take in a single sitting.

"You're not listening," the Priest interjected.

Elric snapped back to attention. "No, no, I am! My apologies, Father."

"Am I boring you, young man?" his tone was stern.
"No, sir."

The Priest continued his sermon: "And thus the Morning Star rose in the east, and with his Divine and perfect will, breathed life into the Archons who created our world and planted the seeds of Wisdom into the hearts of man."

Elric's ears perked up at that statement. "From whence did the Morning Star rise?"

"Excuse me?"

"You said that the Morning Star rose in the east. What did it rise from?"

"The Morning Star predates existence, young man."

"Well, I'm aware of that Father. But that's not what the texts seem to imply. What caused the Morning Star to come into being?"

The Priest looked visibly irritated with the question. "Are you trying to imply that there is a higher being than the Morning Star, young man?" the Priest moved closer to Elric. "As you know, that sort of thought is considered heretical in Alderion."

Elric felt both terrified and cheeky. "No, Father. I'm not trying to imply that in any way. I'm merely trying to put the pieces I've collected through my studies together, and I've yet to come to a satisfying answer."

He paused for a moment to let the Priest process his words before continuing with something of a smirk: "Besides, doesn't most of Lusca follow the path of Ildiachas? It would seem to me that we tolerate quite a lot of heresy in Alderion."

Elric knew at once that he'd made a mistake, even before the switch connected with his left cheek. To strike a Lordling, especially of a high rank, was a rare thing in Alderion. Protocols of respect and deference ran too deep for such a thing to even be thinkable, assuming one wasn't raised by one of the more savage Houses of the realm. Such an action would demand satisfaction, at an honour price far too high than most nobles were willing to pay for such a trifling matter. A clear exception to the rule, of course, were the Priests. A Priest, at his ordination, was thought to obtain a unique connection to the Morning Star. An indelible mark was placed upon his soul, connecting him eternally to that most high and noble spark of the Divine nature that no regular layman could ever hope to attain. In effect, a Priest was a manifestation of the will of the Morning Star in the mortal realms. In all but a very few respects, the Church was above such trivialities as mortal law and custom.

The blow stung his flesh, but the physical pain was nothing

compared to what followed. He turned his head back to look at the Priest. His wrath was apparent, but softening as he waited expectantly for Elric to do what ecclesiastical law demanded of him.

Rage flowed through Elric's veins like white hot fire, but he did his best to wear a neutral expression as he rose to his feet. Placing his feet together and his right hand over his heart, he gave a deep and enduring bow.

"I thank you, Father, for the blessing of your correction. Might I, a lowly sinner, unite my pains to the power of the Archons, and through their prayers of intercession come to know the light of the Morning Star more fully, and become worthy of the forgiveness of you, his Priest and representative here in the mortal realms."

Elric remained in the bow until the Priest touched three fingers to the crown of his head.

"Take well to my correction, Child of the Light of our Lord, and hasten quickly to confession that our Lord may absolve you of your sin and grant you communion with His light eternal."

Taking his cue to leave, Elric turned towards the door, making sure that at all times he avoided direct eye contact with the Priest. That would not be permitted again until he had taken the time to visit the confessional and receive the requisite absolution. His eyes remained downcast even as he took to the halls, knowing full well that even accidental eye contact with a Priest would warrant a further "correction", this time of a much more severe degree. For a moment, he debated simply returning to his room and making further study of the copied papers he still held within his possession, but decided against it. With his schedule, the next chance available to him would likely be more than a week out from that day. Keeping his head down for that length of time seemed immensely unappealing to him, not to mention the loss of status he would incur from among his peers and students. With a sigh, he made his way to the confessional.

It was blessedly emptier than usual, which was nice. While sins were common among students of the Order, wandering to the mercy of the Morning Star with downcast eyes brought with it a special kind of stigma indeed.

It wasn't long until he was brought into the confessional. He sat behind the grated screen and recited the customary words "Bless me oh light of the Morning Star, for I have sinned against thee and done that which is evil in your sight. Turn not your presence from me, nor take your holy luminescence from me."

"Tell me your sins, child."

Elric recounted the incident with the Priest, and threw in a few more incidents throughout the week for good measure. It never hurt within the Order to seem more introspective and contrite; everyone knew that the Priests had a tendency to talk.

"Insubordination is a serious matter indeed," the Priest behind the screen intoned gravely.

Elric nodded, and recited the prayer, "I am deeply sorry for having offended thee, not out of fear of the Darkness but out of a desire to be united unto the Light eternal."

There was silence for a moment, before the Priest finally took in a deep breath and said "I absolve you from your sins. Go in peace, and may the light of the Morning Star guard you eternally against the yawning darkness of the endless chasms."

There was nothing more to be said. Elric rose and existed the confessional, before making his way back to his own quarters. He felt exhausted, and still enraged by his encounter with the Priest. Their power over even the nobility seemed like an affront to him. In his mind, the Priests were nothing more than men who while dedicated to knowledge and study, had no inner strength or renown beyond that. Perhaps he was something of a heretic after all.

Slamming his cell door behind him, he sat down exhausted on his bed before carefully pulling out his copies from a hidden alcove by his headboard. Unfurling the parchment, he read the words written upon it again for what must have been the hundredth time. His Eldar still wasn't the best, but the library had been an enormous help to him in this regard.

And thus in the beginning of time, Sarkas the first emanation of the Divine Will, known for his luminescence as the source of all beauty, took to his role as the fashioner of all. But he sought the crown in all of its glory, and once wrested from the head of grace was thus ever called Yalthabaoth, the seventh archon and the child of chaos by all those who cleaved to the bosom of the first Light as they still despised the world of flesh and blood. The light sleeps within the tombs beneath the Sea. The light will rise. The light will shine again ere the end of all things.

In no other text had Elric been able to find any other mention of these other entities. Rationally, he knew that the text he held in his hands had to be a heresy of some kind, either of the variety long since stamped out by the Church, or a sickening and malicious lie by the followers of Ildiachas who remained in the realms of Alderion. He wouldn't put such a thing past the any of them, and especially of the Banfion usurpers. Yet all the same, the thought that this could be some form of forbidden knowledge, or worse yet, a small fragment of a larger truth, was tantalizing to him. Why else would the librarian bear that look of panic at the mere mention of the contents of these papers? Why, as she fed them into the fire, unaware that Elric had made copies for his own personal study, did she place a consoling hand on his shoulder and say:

"It's best that you put this whole enterprise out of your mind. It's for your own good."

At the time, Elric had agreed, with the ugly inklings of fear placing their fetid seeds within the confines of his heart. Never before in his life had he doubted in any aspect the teachings of the Morning Star. He was born into the Light of the same god as his fathers dating all the way back to Elric the Redwyn, the Black Hawk who saw the love of their god and rejected the poisonous Ildiachas teachings so beloved by House Banfion. The church was infallible, or so he'd been led to believe. So, what was he to make of this?

He set the pages down beside him and rubbed his temples in agony. It would have been better for him to just take the advice of the librarian and set this problem to flames in both his mind and reality once and for all. In that moment, he damned his inquisitive mind to the lowest, most frozen confines of hell.

A knock at his cell door disturbed his excessive ruminations. When no one announced their presence, Elric flew into a blind panic and hid the offending pages back into their secret alcove. If the wrong person saw them, then his migraine stemming from his attempts to figure them out would be the least of his problems. The knock came again, this time more urgent then before. A booming voice called out from behind the door, one which Elric didn't recognize,

"Elric Redwyn," it called.

"One moment," he replied, his voice cracking, "I need to properly dress," he lied as he messed with the hiding place in an attempt to make it seem normal and inconspicuous to the unassuming eye.

"Open the door," the voice boomed again.

Out of time now, Elric said a silent prayer to the archons to intercede on his behalf before rushing to the door and swinging it open. His heart sank into his feet.

Standing before him were three Knights of the Order, along with two guardsmen of Alderion. The clasps that normally held the swords of Knights in their scabbards, at least while on holy ground, were undone.

"Come with us," the man who had been knocking said, "You have been summoned by the Master and are to attend to him at once."

"Gentlemen," Elric turned on his charms, with a small dash of magical glamour, "surely this is unnecessary. I am his personal pupil, after all. A simple messenger would have been enough to make me drop everything and rush to his side."

"You can come with us quietly, or we can do this the hard way," the Knight told him, placing his dominant hand across his body and onto his sword, "it's your choice."

There really wasn't any choice to be made at all. "Let's go," Elric said.

CIARAN

Ciaran stumbled into his quarters, already half drunk but drained from his day and desperate to sit in silence with a flagon of spiced wine. The negotiations, though long and intellectually dry, weren't the worst part. Not by a country mile. Rather, it was the rigid protocol by which everything had to be done. Introductions alone seemed to take an eternity, and if Ciaran had to endure one more sympathetic nod after explaining his lack of a Lordly title, he couldn't be sure what he would do. At any rate, it would most certainly be offensive to any poor soul who happened to be caught in the crossfire.

He stumbled over to the table where the servants had set the flagon ahead of his arrival. It was both highly convenient and shameful that they'd acclimated to his habits as swiftly as they had. All the same, it was a welcome sight. He poured himself a hearty glass, which he drained swiftly, and then refilled it before sitting down on one of the couches nearby the window. The breeze coming off the sea felt good on his skin. For a moment, he just allowed himself to unfocus and be lulled into a mild trance by the sounds of the ocean and sea birds.

A knock at the door snapped him out of his brief moment of peace. "Enter," he called out, before taking another sip of his wine. To his relief, it was only Willem who entered.

Ciaran stood up to meet him, "My friend! How are you? Come, get yourself some refreshment."

Ciaran poured an additional glass for Ciaran before both of them sat back down on the couch. "I presume this isn't wholly a social call," Ciaran at last stated flatly.

"I'm afraid not," Willem said as he produced a sealed envelope from his breast pocket and handed it to Ciaran.

He opened it, and took a brief moment to read it. With a high, he flung the paper down upon a nearby table. "Of course," he rubbed his temples.

"What did it say?" Willem inquired. Without a word, Ciaran handed the paper to his friend for him to read on his own.

"Oh," Willem breathed.

"I can't say that I'm surprised," Ciaran took a large swig of his drink and immediately poured himself another. By now, Willem knew better than to tell the man to slow down. It had a tendency to do far more harm than good. When Ciaran wanted to talk, he would.

A few moments of silence was all that it took. Ciaran at last opened up.

"I can't say I'm surprised that she'd do this. What shocks me is her lack of decorum. The bitch couldn't even wait until my mother's body was cold to make her move, it seems."

Willem filled his glass for him, ostensibly inviting him to continue.

Ciaran didn't need the encouragement. He took the glass, and went on: "Not to say that I trust this Lord Starkfall. He's not much older than me, and has only very recently come into the Lordship in his own right. But, we take our friends, false or no, where we can find them, don't we?"

"I'm not sure I follow," Willem said.

Ciaran smiled, "That's fine. Can you be a lad and fetch me my stationary? It's high time we pulled some tricks of our own."

Wordless, Willem replied and fetched the requested items. Like a whirlwind, he set to work carefully composing multiple letters. Each letter appeared as though it were penned by the hand of someone else. Willem stopped him to ask:

"Have you done this before?"

"Let's not ask questions we don't necessarily want to know the answers to, hm?" came the reply.

They sat in silence as Ciaran worked, with Willem occasionally refilling his drink. The work went on for some hours, with a brief respite coming when the governess of the Lady Shirra knocked at the door to announce the arrival of the princess. In an instant, the rage in Ciaran's eyes was gone as he rose to greet his younger sister and hear all about the intricacies of the young child's day.

He'd been right to bring her along. The young girl had blossomed in her time at the Sasanan court; going from her shy and unassuming nature into that of a bubbling beacon of brightness, like quicksilver on the cusp of womanhood. Even as boring trade negotiations threatened to bring Ciaran to an early grave, Shirra's brief appearances had always been enough to endear him, and the Realm he represented, to even the stuffiest of foreign Lords. The enterprise at the table was all but abandoned as Shirra, and her assigned governess, regaled him with tales. Willem couldn't help but smile at the child's exuberance himself.

But like all candles that burned twice as bright, she soon grew tired and had to retire to bed. Rather than allow the governess to take over, Ciaran simply dismissed her for the night and placed the child in her chambers himself. "Please return in the morning," were his only instructions to her.

And with that, the work resumed. By the time Ciaran at last set down his quill, the inkwell had been drained dry and the sun had long set below the horizon on the ocean. He went to refill his glass, only to realize that the wine too was gone. He moved over towards the door and rang a bell to summon an attendant, before sitting back down in his chair and rubbing his aching wrist. All told, there were approximately ten letters of varying lengths written up and ready to be sent off to their respective recipients.

"We'll need to make some seals, but I think this will work," Ciaran at last gave himself the space to breathe.

"What's the plan then?" Willem felt safe enough to ask. The two men stayed quiet for a moment as the attendant arrived to deliver two additional flagons of spiced wine and a small cask of rum. "Thank you," they both said in unison, as they waited for the attendant to leave.

Alone yet again, Ciaran poured them both a drink and smiled to himself. "Maeve Lothric happens to be married to my uncle, the poor fool. Whoever thought marrying one brother to a Redwyn and the other to a Banfion made for a recipe for peace and prosperity was perhaps a bigger drunkard and failure than I am."

Willem went to interrupt, but stopped as Ciaran began speaking yet again, "Regardless of that idiocy, she likes to think that she's smarter than she is. She didn't account for letters detailing her plans reaching my eyes. As I said, I don't trust Lord Starkfall. I scarcely know the man. At best, he's playing both sides and attempting to curry favor with whomever might happen to win, at worst he's a violent fool. But either way, I can use him for my purposes."

Ciaran continued, "These first three letters are intended for the largest trading houses in Sasana for House Lothric, Redwyn, and the Imperial Court respectively. Where the Imperial Court may be able to cut Lusca off from the rest of Alderion, it seems my dear aunt has failed to take into account our international contacts, which the Imperial Court frankly has little to no influence over short of a war. I don't even think the Redwyn's would be that foolhardy in their quest for a power grab."

"What about the rest?"

Ciaran smiled, "The Redwyn's like to operate under the assumption that they're the only house with friends in high places, that mine is run by nothing but pariah women with more money than sense. These four are addressed to those friends, targeting those things which they care about that will be dispensed with should Lusca come under higher influence from the Imperial Court, let alone this asinine attempt at a Redwyn coup. Be it religion, money, or the simple fact that they have something to lose should the favor of House Banfion suddenly be withdrawn, these will be the easiest houses to bring on side that happen to wield the most power compared to my own."

"And the final two?"

"Oh, those are simple," Ciaran smiled, "One is a directive to my father to immediately cease all deliveries of food to Lothric lands. While I'm sure it will pain him to cause any suffering to my uncle and my cousins, I don't think starving out the Lothric's will be a permanent arrangement that gets anywhere near to that point. What I'm counting on, in fact, is my uncle becoming so enraged by my aunt's actions and the rift with his dear brother that he effectively places my aunt on house arrest. Truly, she didn't think her actions through."

"That leaves one more,"

"It's a fake letter to Elric Redwyn."

"Why would you send something like that?"

"Presumably she's doing all of this to place him on my Lady Sister's throne. I want to nip that in the bud. I can't say that I know the man. In truth, I don't. But last I heard, Lord Alaric had sent him to the Order of the Morning Star to learn the secrets of their magic. I doubt that would happen if he weren't a man of at least some intellect. Regardless of the bluster of House Redwyn, I don't think any actions short of a civil war will place them on the throne of Lusca, and I think if this Elric is intelligent enough to learn magic, he must know that on some level. Further, and this is conjecture on my part, I get the feeling that there is little love lost between him and my aunt. It shouldn't be hard to make him adverse to any plans of hers. To that end, I'm simply going to pose as my uncle Aengus. I will make it clear to Elric that my dear Lady wife has lost her mind with grief due to her inability to grant me another heir, and that he ought to disregard any mad ravings he might already have received from her. I simply don't think he'll have enough affection in his heart for her to send any further letters to confirm the situation."

Willem took a sip of his drink, "And you think this will work?"

Ciaran shrugged, "Any part of this plan could fail at any juncture. That's why I've tried my best here to cover any eventualities. If even one part of this succeeds, I'm sure it will throw enough of a spanner into things to at least buy my sister some time. Though in truth, I'm not entirely sure how she'll elect to deal with this. She tends to be somewhat conniving, but I don't put it past her to take Lusca to war to assert her place."

Willem sighed, "Let's hope it doesn't come to that. The Mountain Clans would almost certainly take advantage of chaos like that."

"They would," Ciaran agreed, "So let's hope it doesn't come to that." He rose to his feet, unsteady now with the effects of the wine, and reached out a hand to the back of his chair to steady himself. He gestured at Willem, "You know, it's at times like these that I'm somewhat glad that my family doesn't give the throne to men. Can you imagine the stress of having to play off half an empire against one other, all of the time, all while having to look like a vision of Elven beauty? No thanks," he took a sip, "I'd rather work behind the scenes and enjoy my life. Or what's left of it, at any rate."

Willem smiled, "Well, I'm glad you worked that out for yourself." He rose to leave.

"Wait," Ciaran called out, his speech now excessively slurred, "Sit back down. Or have you forgotten? You still owe me tales of the Mountain Clans."

MAEVE

Maeve smiled to herself as she finished composing another letter to her nephew. He had yet to respond to any of her correspondence, but she chalked that up largely to his days being more busy than not. The Order of the Morning Star was a rigorous institution, after all. Sealing the letter with the seal of House Lothric, she handed it off to her maid "Send this to the Order, please."

She made her way to the main hall, smiling to herself. For the first time in many years, she felt confident and empowered. After all of the embarrassing failures of her house, they were now on the cusp of their ultimate victory. She doubted sincerely that the new "Queen" of Lusca would have either the experience of the wherewithal to fight against a multi pronged attack from multiple houses, let alone the might of the Imperial Court itself.

Upon entering the main hall, what she saw there gave her a bit of a start. Sitting before the fire, a letter in his hand, was her husband.

"Maeve," he called out to her, his voice grave, "come. Sit with me for a moment."

"Of course, my Lord," she smiled, sat, and took his hand. "What troubles you?"

Rather than look his wife in the eye, Aengus simply unfurled the letter and began to read from it:

"You are my brother, and your children are as dear to me as my own blood. However, the actions of your Lady wife cannot be allowed to stand. Until such time as the loyalty of House Lothric can be assured, I, Midir, in the name Roisin, Lady of Lusca, Queen of the Snowstone Mountains and the Sunset Isles beyond the Sea, do hereby withdraw the protection of the High Lordship of Lusca from your house. I name you anathema, and strip from you all incomes, rents, and shipments of food from her realm. Upon such time as you are willing to meet with your Liege and re-pledge your loyalty, no house within her Realm may trade or do any business with your own. Do better, dear brother."

Aengus threw the paper in his wife's face. "Explain yourself, now!" he roared.

Maeve was awestruck. "I-I'm not sure what he's talking about. There must be some mistake. I'm sure if you were to write to your brother, this could all be straightened out."

"It's too late for that," Aengus rose, his presence large and terrifying. For a split second his face shifted to a mask of calm, before he struck out with his left hand and connected it with Maeve's cheek, sending the woman falling to the ground.

"A woman who would risk her own children for ambition," he spat and motioned for a guard. "Take her away. I have a trip to prepare for."

The guards moved to hoist an awestruck Maeve to her feet. She screamed as they dragged her away towards the dungeons of the castle she called her home.

DIARMID

It was high noon when at long last the ancient barrows of Saelmere came into sight. They weren't as ostentatious as he might have expected. With the might of the family and their pedigree, he had been expecting something far more elaborate. Instead, the barrows of Saelmere were nothing more at first sight than a collection of hills overgrown by winter lilies. Their bright blue - which matched Lady Roisin's eyes, he noticed – contrasted sharply with the iridescent, undisturbed white snow. The gentle mounds looks like pale, white flesh adorned with dripping sapphires. The entrances were subdued and hard to spot in comparison to the tombs of other great and mighty lords. The doors, as they were, were simple, unadorned stone slabs supported by ebony wood. On either side of each door were basket shaped holders for torches. They torches were only ever lit for the recently deceased, to guide their spirit through to the afterlife rather than leaving it upon this earth to haunt the living. No torches were lit, at least as far as Diarmid could see.

He dismounted his horse, patting the mare as he thought deeply about how he wanted to handle the situation. There were numerous barrows to check, each of them sprawling underground complexes in their own right. Some of them, of course, could be safely ruled out. The larger hill mounds were newer, less weathered by time and the harsh Luscan winters. He doubted that the Banfions would plunder their own tombs to retrieve an amulet long buried with one of their matriarchs for the sake of putting it somewhere nicer.

No, he thought, that could only leave the older tombs closer to the back of the field, and that was a much more daunting prospect that the simple earthen mounds before him. Even in the age of Awen and Eoghan, to say nothing of the Lords and Ladies of this place beforehand, not much distinction had been made between a burial crypt and a brutal military transport tunnel. The places were labyrinths, even more so than the alleged tunnels beneath Saelmere itself. This was by design, of course. Should the enemy find their way into those ancient tunnels, they were just as like as to get lost and gradually starve to death in the dank, dark earth as they were to happen upon anything of use. Diarmid shuddered at the idea that he too might meet the same fate as those who once tried to invade Lusca and overthrow the Winter Queen.

He stared for a moment at the fading light of day, and felt his courage go out of him. "It's getting cold," he made a quick excuse, "and it'll only be colder in the barrows themselves. I say we make camp and set forth in the morning."

Devon and Tuirean looked at their Lord with skepticism before shrugging their shoulders and starting at making their nightly camp. Diarmid helped, as much as his friends would allow, busying his racing thoughts with the rhythmic strike of hammer on tent stake into freezing earth. Just as the sun shrank below the horizon, Cian got a new fire started and Geoff brought forth the remainder of the venison he'd hunted on their first night out.

The smell of searing, salted meat was a welcome distraction. Diarmid chewed his portion pensively, washing it down with some of their rationed mead. The inter-mixture of honey and salt was something to be savoured, and something he knew he would not be experiencing again for some time. Who knew how long it would take to search all these barrows? On some level, Diarmid was starting to wonder whether or not Roisin had sent him on this quest not as a grand romantic gesture of his affections, but as a subtle form of rejection.

His friends chatted together in their usual, boisterous way, weaving tangled webs of their dreamed future glories. After all, to be one of the men who found a lost amulet of legend would be enough to make each of them desirable and worthy of a knighthood in their own right. Diarmid tries his best to engage, but after a while resigned himself to his silent contemplation. He was first to retire for the night, electing to take the final watch of the night and took upon himself the obligation of the morning preparations. The idea being, of course, that a good night's rest would soothe his anxieties and leave him all the braver come the dawn.

Oh, what a fool he was.

His sleep was fitful at best, and plagued by nightmares. In his dreams, he entered the barrows alone, his torch the only light to guide him as he ventured all the further into that cursed realm of the dead. The light of life, of the sun, faded behind him fast as he went deeper and deeper into the earth, and with the fading of the light came the fading of heat and of warmth. He saw his breath crystallize in the air in front of him as he ventured deeper. As it grew darker and darker, he couldn't help but shake the eerie feeling that small eyes were watching him from the shadowy crevices of the earthen walls. The dark of the earth and the feeling of being watched grew more oppressive, and Diarmid swore that the shadows were even beginning to swallow the light of the fire on his torch. When he heard the shuffling footsteps behind him, he broke into a frantic run, hitting the walls around and him tripping into damp mud as he went. The torch went out, and with that final fading of the light came the crashing open of his emotional floodgates. He screamed, so loud that his muscles tore in his throat, and broke into a frenzied run, no longer caring where he was going or taking any care to keep track of where he was going. The shuffled steps behind him sped up, and when the cold dead flesh grasped his arm and yanked him backwards, he heard an audible moan.

Diarmid woke with a start, screaming as he drew the dagger he kept as a sidearm. Cian jumped backwards in surprise, holding his hands up to avoid the slashing motion of Diarmid's blade.

"Diarmid, Diarmid!" he shouted, more forcefully on the second repetition, "you were screaming in your sleep. It's just me, Cian." He lowered his voice to be more friendly and soothing, "Besides, it's time for you to take the watch."

Cian retired to his bedding to sleep. Diarmid groaned and forcefully rubbed his eyes. The dream had been so vivid and lifelike that his heart was still pounding in his chest, and his ears rung with anxious tension. He looked outside. It was still dark, with no hint of the oncoming morning light.

He rose and dressed, securing his cloak and his sword to his person. Then, he set to packing his portion of their camp. This wasn't required of him, but it would make things easier once everyone else awoke. Then, he simply grabbed a drink and sat by the fire. The warmth of the flames were a gentle comfort, chasing away the chilled demons of the nightmare that still haunted his thoughts. Every now and then, the normal sounds of the winter forest at night made him look up with alarm, gripping the hilt of his sword with a white knuckled force that surprised him. He's been in battle before. He'd killed men stronger than himself. He wondered aloud, "When did I turn into a craven, green boy?"

In time, the sky began to lighten. First the black of night turned to a gentle purple, then velvet blue, until at last he saw the inkling of the pale grey of the dawn on the horizon, and with it the pinks, reds, and oranges of the rising sun and genesis of a new day. Their breakfast was to be simple, just some salted bacon they'd brought with them as provision. The smell of sizzling meat roused the men, and Diarmid felt a simple joy at having human company.

They ate, and he joked and bantered with them as he had before, as though nothing had ever been bothering him to begin with. The food, which on a normal day he would be forced to admit wasn't very good even by the standards of a hedge knight, tasted to him as though it were prepared by the finest chefs trained for the kitchens of the High King himself. The dawn brought with it joy, and a renewed sense of their purpose here.

They packed up their camp, still enjoying one other's company. At last, it was up to Diarmid to choose a barrow for them to check first. Something about the one nearest to their camp seemed to call to him. It was old, incredibly so. The mound seemed to be sinking into the earth around it, and the entrance didn't look stable by any means. And yet, it called to him all the same. Lighting their torches from their campfire, then men gave a mighty heave and wrenched the stone slab from its moorings. The structural integrity of the barrow didn't look so bad from the inside. Ducking their heads beneath the sinking entry way, they bore forth.

They only had to duck for a brief time. As they went deeper, down and down into the dark earth, the roof above them seemed to heighten and then level off. Each man would still easily hit their head off the ceiling should they feel the need to jump, but at least their backs ceased to scream at the strain. They walk two abreast, with Diarmid and Cian taking up the point, and Tuirean taking the rear guard. The barrow was quiet, and as it grew colder and darker, Diarmid couldn't help but feel that night time anxiety begin to creep up on him once again.

"How deep do these places go?" he heard Devon ask from behind him.

"It depends," Diarmid answered, "Some of the great Winter Queens had elaborate complexes built that can easily go on for miles. Others just had simple burial mounds. It really just depends on when they were built, and for which Lady. I imagine if this is where we'll find the tomb of Awen, it'll be rather large."

Cian added, "That's not even taking into account that most of these barrows probably overlap one other, either by a mistake that the Banfion's will never admit to, by design, or simply because of the passage of time and the natural collapse of untended tunnels."

Diarmid gave his assent, "That's another thing we'll have to be careful of. No one maintains these places, especially since the Banfion's started to regularly cremate their dead and no longer use them as military forts. If you feel the ground start to give way, we're gonna have to run."

"Lovely," he heard Tuirean spit dismissively.

"Wait," Geoff stopped and whispered suddenly.
Everyone else froze. "You don't – you don't feel shifting earth, do you?" Devon asked plaintively.

"No, no," Geoff whispered, "Did you guys hear that?"

"Hear what? Tuirean said aloud, only to be summarily shushed by the rest of the men.

They listened for what seemed like a minor eternity. The wind above them howled, and if they listened carefully, they could hear dripping, standing water elsewhere in the complex. But that wouldn't have been enough to stop Geoff dead in his tracks.

Diarmid listened carefully, straining his ears against the oppressive silence.

At last, he heard it. The shuffling of feet against dry earth near by.

The blood drained from his heart, and fear replaced the void where there had once been warmth and optimism. Before his eyes, his nightmare flashed anew.

They were not alone down here.

And something was very, very wrong.

ROISIN

Roisin's eyes snapped open. The air around her was cold, and her extremities felt numb. It took her a moment to realize that she was no longer in the tunnels beneath her castle – the overcast skies with fat snowflakes falling down upon her face was enough evidence of that. She rose to her feet, shaking some of the snow from the folds of her dress.

"There she is!" a voice cried out from the distance.

A contingent of guards and stewards raced towards her, their looks of concern etched into their faces. A lady is waiting rushed to place a shawl around her shoulders.

"My lady! Where have you been? We've been so worried." she raved.

Roisin wrapped her fingers, chilled to the bone, in the folds of the cloth and blew gently into it in an attempt to warm them. A knight took note of this and wrapped her in his fur lined cloak instead.

"May I?" he offered.

Roisin nodded and the knight swooped her off her feet and carried her back towards the castle, towards warmth and safety. He brought her to the main hall and placed her in a chair next to a roaring fire. She didn't dare remove the clothes and furs she'd been covered with, not yet at any rate. A maid brought her a glass of warmed cider, and she felt as though she had little choice but to hold it through the cloth, so hot did it feel against her frozen fingers. The flurry of activity around her seemed distant and far away compared to the ruminations in her own mind. The sounds around her seemed to be a distant din, her ears ringing from stress. It had clearly been some time between the events of the tunnels and her awakening. What frightened her to the bone was the fact that she bore within her mind no memory of any of it.

In time, she found the dexterity of her hands slowly returning, and though they still burned with the chill of an internalized ice, she found it easier to grasp the glass of hot cider. The alcohol in the drink warmed her insides, and brought a sense of calm to her troubled spirit. Soon, she began to feel normal again. The heat from the fire and the furs grew bothersome rather than comforting, and she quickly found herself removing them.

"Are you alright, my Lady?" the knight asked of her.

"Yes, Sir, I am," Roisin smiled at him, hoping to put him at ease. He placed his left fist over his heart in a sign of respect, and withdrew.

As if on cue, Edwin took his entrance into his presence. With the appropriate bow, he begged for an audience with his Queen.

"My Lady," he entreated.

"Edwin," she touched him in a sign of acknowledgment. "What is it that you require of me?"

"If you are feeling up to it, my lady," his voice croaked, "there is a matter that requires your attention in the South Hall. A rider from the high seat of Alderion has come bearing a message that requires your attention."

Roisin snapped to attention, a chill running down her spine. A message from the Court of the High King was a rare thing indeed, and generally only came about during the most serious of circumstances. The High King was unconcerned with pedestrian matters like the crowning of a new monarch, and Roisin knew too well that there had been little love lost between him and her late mother. She had met the High King once when she had still been a young girl, come forth to the grand capitol to learn from her mother as she entreated the highest Lordship in the land for military assistance against the Mountain Clans. As ostensibly a vassal equal to any other, it was Lady Eafyn's sovereign right to do so. After all, part of the deal when a Kingdom joined the ranks of the Imperial Sovereignty was the expectation of military assistance against those who would make incursion into a land's sovereign borders.

But prejudices ran deeper than agreements signed in the blood of her forebears, as Lady Eafyn would be swift to find out. Roisin still remembered her mother's face turned to a mask of stone as she challenged the High King:

"Would your answer be the same if the request had come from a Redwyn?" she asked in a tone so icy it made the Snowstone Mountains themselves seem like a roaring fire in one's hearth.

"How dare you!" the High King roared, fully cognizant of the true depths of the challenge he'd been given by a Lord who he clearly viewed as an unworthy, and perhaps illegitimate woman.

"How dare I indeed," Lady Eafyn retorted, her tone still level and cold. "Perhaps I might dare to go further. My realm does control the most profitable rivers and farmland in this farce of an Empire, after all."
The threat could not have been clearer, at which point the High King's own Lady sought to intervene, placing a hand on the arm of her raging husband.

"Lady Eafyn, you come from a most noble line indeed. Are there not many famed Shieldmaidens within the ranks of your ancestry? Surely some common rabble from the mountains cannot be causing your realm that much trouble. Nonetheless, I'm sure my dear Lord Husband could spare a few warriors, though it will take several moons to muster fighting men worthy of your own considerable armies."

The High King, who had by then come aware of his senses, assented. Lady Eafyn simply turned and walked out of the hall, without even entreating Roisin to follow her. They rode back to Lusca that very same night, with the impassioned ranting of her mother serving to keep Roisin awake in her carriage as they moved at a break neck pace.

The promised warriors never did come. And the incursions by the Mountain Clans continued until her mother was left in a state worse than the eternal sleep of death.

In many ways, the High King of Alderion had killed her mother. He had to know that. Which chilled Roisin all the more. The memories she had of him did not belie a man prone to remorse or humility.

By now Roisin had far outpaced her haggard Steward, and she hoped that he would forgive her impropriety, though in all honesty none existed at this point if the order of precedence were to be followed to the letter. She raced into the South Hall, blowing back the doors with a well placed push, startling all those who were within. Upon beholding the visage of their Queen, the Luscan men and women all rose to their feet and variously curtsied or bowed in acknowledgment. The Alderion rider stood out imminently in his refusal to do so. Roisin strode up to him, her head held high in a stature befitting that of a Queen. She stared the rider down with the same glare of Snowstone ice that she'd once seen grace the face of her mother, resolving not to back down until the rider submitted.

"My Lady," he addressed her, equally stone faced. "I come bearing a message from your Lord, the High King of all Alderion."

Roisin refused to acknowledge him until due respect was given.

At last, the dam within the man broke. He blinked repeatedly, "Forgive me, my Lady, I forget my manners." He sank into a deep, respectful bow. Rising from his supplication, he handed a sealed letter to Roisin. Without a word, she took it and inspected the seal. It was that of the High King, unbroken. Barring any instruction, it was unlikely that this rider knew the contents. Though his disrespect of her left that in some manner of doubt. Breaking the seal, she unfurled the paper and read the message it contained,

Roisin, Lady of Lusca, Queen of the Snowstone Mountains and the Sunset Isles beyond the Sea,

It saddened us greatly to hear of the final passing of your dear mother, Lady Eafyn. It is always a tragedy to hear of the end of a Lord of our realms. May the Light of the Morning Star shine upon her spirit, and grant her repose. Further, we feel compelled to congratulate you on at last coming into your own as Queen. You have made a fair steward of your mother's realm, and we are confident that you will continue to serve faithfully in your role. We are most glad indeed that you have avoided a regency.

However now that Lusca is under most competent leadership, we are afraid that a matter has arisen.

Due to the impropriety of your Lady mother some years prior, we are afraid that at present we can no longer allow other Realms within Alderion to trade with thine own. Surely this matter can be rectified most fortuitously, and to that end we request your presence at our pleasure so that you might swear fealty to us and submit to the Order of the Morning Star.

To this end, another matter has arisen. We have requested a retinue of your druids to accompany you and settle once and for all the matter of female succession. We are aware that this has been the practice of House Banfion for some millennia, and it would be loathe upon us to change such a thing without cause. However, as our realms grow in faith, the question of your legitimacy must be settled before tribunal to assure peace in our time and among our people.

As such, we request your presence forthwith. Please take any time you need to make preparation, but we request that you appear before us within the next moon.

Roisin's hands shook with rage as she read the paper. It was at this time that Edwin at last made his appearance in the hall, his countenance changing at once as soon as he saw her expression. She glanced up to notice the flash of a smirk from the rider.

"Thank you for your message," she said, coolly. "I'm sure your master will reward you most heartily when all is said and done."

"I take my leave then," he said.

Roisin gestured to a knight, who drew his sword. "I'm afraid not," she explained. "You see, I know things are far different in the capitol. But far be it for any Lord of Lusca to leave their realm at the behest of another without some form of... assurances."

The rider attempted to run for the door and was subdued by the knight in short order. The rider struggled in vain.

"You can't do this!" he screamed, much like a child.

"I already have," Roisin retorted. "Perhaps you should consider the master you choose to serve, if your safety is of such importance to you. Why are you so fearful, my Lord?" she asked, "Surely your great High King will assure your safety. It's not as if he's ever betrayed a vassal or servant of his realm before, now has he?"

Her facade had fallen and the rage in her voice was clear. "You will be treated humanely and released upon my safe return to my realm, of that I can assure you."

Edwin, who had some idea of what was going on, motioned for Roisin to hand him the letter. She did so, and watched his face grow grave and crestfallen. "It seems not even death can calm the malice of His Lordship," he sighed.

"Ready my horse and as many knights and men at arms as can be mustered on short notice." Roisin commanded.

"Do you mean to go to war, my Lady?" Edwin asked, the fear on his face quite palpable indeed.

"That depends solely on the actions of our Lord," she said the last word with venom, "but it doesn't hurt to be prepared."

ELRIC

The guards took formation around him, with the three Knights of the Order taking the point in front of Elric, and the Guardsmen of Alderion following behind. Elric racked his brain for the reason behind such a show of force. While the Priests were known to talk among themselves about the various sins and transgressions of their congregants, it was strictly forbidden for them to divulge such things to anyone who was not themselves a confessor. While the Master was, in technicality, a Priest, as he was not himself an active confessor, his sin should not have been divulged to him. To do so in and of itself would have been a sin, one which could only be expunged from the confessors soul through the trial of the rack. The extreme nature of the penance was enough to keep most Priests from ever dreaming of breaking the seal.

His thoughts turned to the librarian, but he doubted her involvement. If she were willing to turn him over as a heretic, then why would she have taken such cares to destroy the original papers and swear Elric to secrecy? More to the point, revealing him would have by extension revealed herself. By destroying the papers, she knowingly and willfully protected a potential heretic. No, it couldn't have been her.

The only other possibility was that a steward had discovered the papers within the alcove during a routine cleaning of his cell and reported them. But if that were the case, then would they not have reasonably removed the offending material from its hiding place as evidence?

Despite his guilty conscience, there was also the possibility that this had nothing to do with the papers at all, but more so to do with the incessant questions Elric had been asking of anyone who might give him an answer without revealing the reason behind his queries. While an inquisitive nature was encouraged within the Order, some lines of questioning were simply off limits. They were lines of thought that revealed, by their very nature, that someone was questioning the foundations of the Faith. He prayed to every Archon and the Morning Star himself that this was the reason, and the show of force was merely the Master's way of underscoring his deep concern for his star pupil.

They made their way through the meandering halls of the Order until they came to the spiral staircase that led far into the Heavens into the personal quarters of the Master himself. Elric had never been in this room; all of his pastoral care and instruction had up until now been conducted in various chapels and en-suites of the library, sometimes even in his own cell.

The guards stopped, with the main Knight opening the door and directing Elric to go upstairs. "We shall remain here," he told him. "You have been instructed to make your way upstairs."

It was not a request. Elric nodded and entered the stairway.

The ascent towards the Master's quarters filled him with unspeakable dread. In every other instance where the Master had sought to quell his foolish, boy like ways and mold him into a man that his House could be proud of, he had done so in the guise of a concerned yet stern father. Someone that Elric had never truly had. It's what had engendered the enduring loyalty and affection he'd held for the man, and why his conscience was all the more tormented by the doubts he was now having. Every step felt like a punch in the gut, and he could feel his heart beating in the veins of his neck. At long last, he came to the large, oak door that separated the stairway from the Master's apartments. Taking in a deep breath, which did little to calm his nerves, Elric knocked on the door.

The silence seemed to last for an eternity even as the report of his knocking echoed through the stone hall. At long last: "Enter."

The powerful door creaked as it opened. Elric wasn't sure what he was expecting, but what he saw shocked him all the same. The Master's personal apartments were nothing like what they'd been rumoured to be. Rather than edifices of silver and gold adorning walls filled with priceless art, the room was rather modest. The odd painting could be seen on the walls, but they were really no different than what one could find in any of the other halls throughout the keep. A fire roared in the hearth at the far end, it's warmth a welcome sensation and sight. The Master stood there beside it, his face grave and filled with concern. He motioned at the chairs next to the fire. "Sit," he commanded. Elric did.

The Master walked away for a moment towards his personal kitchens. The fact that he used them at all was another surprise. Previous Holy Father's, as they were known outside of their role of instructing Clerics and students of the sacred arts like himself, were known for their banquets but far less so for their culinary prowess. As he was thinking on it, the Master returned, sporting a flagon and two horn cups for spiced, heated wine. He sat down and set down the flagon and cups on a nearby table before pouring a portion of warmed alcohol into both cups and handing one to Elric, who accepted. The Master took a sip of his own wine, implicitly granting Elric permission to do the same. The warmth of the wine and the flush it brought to his flesh was comforting in its own right, though by now his anxiety had been mostly drowned out by confusion.

"Relax," the Master told him. Elric took another sip and tried his best.

They sat in silence like that for some time, until Elric had finished his cup of wine. Without another word, the Master poured them both seconds. When he was confident that Elric was no longer in a panic, he at last spoke.

"You've been asking questions,"

Elric's eyes must have betrayed some fear, "Relax, son. You're not in any trouble. I just wish to talk with you."

"Then why did you send the Knights to collect me?" Elric blurted out, despite himself. "I would have come at the word of a messenger,"

"Oh, them?" the Master laughed, which put Elric a bit at ease. "You're right, I should have sent a messenger. No, my boy, they aren't for you. Not necessarily, at any rate. They're to accompany you on a task I wish for you to complete for me after our conversation here today."

All at once, he felt his tense muscles loosen in relief.

"Now, about those questions," the Master said, getting comfortable in his seat. "I'm aware that some weeks ago you attempted to seek an audience with me about something. I deeply apologize that at the time I was too busy with other matters to attend your needs. That is a personal fault of mine. I pledged personally to your Lord Grandfather to take responsibility for your education as a future Lord and King, and I'm afraid that I have been derelict in that duty."

Elric tried to protest, but the Master cut him off.

"It is the responsibility of a good shepherd not only to guide his flock, but to retrieve those of his sheep when they become lost or uncertain along the path. You have grown mightily along that path, and will make some day a fine leader, magus, and King. But you are not yet yourself a master. There are secrets that you cannot be privy to. Not out of malice, but out of the love the Morning Star shows to his children. He does not wish to burden us with that which we're ill equipped to understand. It would simply cause you more pain to receive those answers now. But, I think my son, you know that already."

"I-I think so," Elric replied, not entirely sure that they were on the same page.

The Master poured him another cup, even though Elric had not asked for it. "The librarian told me everything, young man."

His bowels turned to ice before the Master continued.

"She told me about how you failed to understand the papers Johanne put together for you. This does not surprise me at all, and he has been sternly reprimanded for his failures as a steward in my service. What she brought me from your effects was a seventh level spell. Does that sound accurate to you?"

Silently thanking all of the archons and any other spirit that might be listening, Elric replied "Yes, I couldn't figure out why my mana wouldn't respond to the Eldar I was speaking to direct it."

The Master smiled at him, "You are a skilled magus, Elric, but even the most talented among us requires instruction and guidance. Those lessons will be taught to you in time, my son. Far sooner than you might have given yourself credit for these past weeks. Ponder no more upon it. You have my personal assurance that I will instruct you myself in these matters after you have completed the task that I shall set before you. In fact, it is one that you will be most interested in. Our High King wishes to finally settle the question of the succession to your ancestral homeland of Lusca.

Elric's back stiffened in attention, the creeping intoxication instantly forgotten. He only realized that he'd begun holding his breath when the Master at last spoke again:

"I'm sending you to two places. The seventh level of the library, under my special authorization. You will retrieve for me the texts written here," he handed Elric a list. "Additionally, I will require you to act as my personal envoy between the Order and the High Keep until such time as the tribunal to decide the question of the Lordship of Lusca is decided. To help facilitate this, the High King himself has sent guards to accompany you. Though, I believe you've already met. No matter, they will ensure that you will pass freely and without hindrance while you perform your work as my personal steward, a position which you may be entitled to keep if you perform your tasks well. After you retrieve the texts, you will deliver this message to His Imperial Majesty. Can you do these things for me, son?"

Elric took the sealed scroll in his hand and bowed solemnly. "I won't let you down," he stated.

The Master smiled at him, "I know you won't, my dear boy."

Elric collected himself and the papers before heading down the stairs. The chief knight greeted him warmly: "You've received your instructions then, I gather?" he inquired.

Elric nodded. "We'll need to go to the library first. Though I have a request, if you don't mind?"

The guardsmen looked at him, expectant of their instructions.

"If you could, I'd have you wait outside on the general grounds for me. I'm aware that you have your orders, but you'll draw far more attention to me inside the grounds of the Order than you will outside of it, and I'd like to maintain my repute within its ranks."

The chief gave a bow, "As you wish, my Lord," as his party departed.

Elric made his way to the library, yet something caught his eye before he made his way to the stairs leading to the higher floors. He spied before him what must have been the most beautiful woman he'd ever seen in his life. Braided, snow white hair stretched down to the small of her back, contrasting mightily with her raven black cloak. Even from her profile, the brilliance of her sapphire blue eyes took his breath away. And better yet, she looked lost.

After smoothing out his surcoat and hair, he tapped her on the shoulder. "Do you need some assistance, my Lady?"

DIARMID

The blood of each man froze in his veins as their group listened to the sound of shuffling grow closer. They'd moved deeper into the tunnels, in the vain hope that the noises they were hearing were nothing more than the shuffling of feet above from mourners come to visit their long deceased ancestors. That had proven to be a lapse in judgment. They didn't possess a map to the barrows. This meant, of course, that their only means out of the sprawling complex was now behind them – in the path of the shuffling noises that were rapidly gaining on them. Diarmid shut his eyes tight for a moment, in an attempt to force his mind to think faster. The noises grew closer.

There was no other option.

"Run!" he drew his sword and broke forth through the tunnel. His friends followed suit and came up behind him fast. The shuffled walking noise turned into a shuffled run, and a low moan escaped the lips of whatever was chasing them.

Cian was oddly the first to lose his nerve. He screamed and pushed forward, panicking and doing his best to get away. He dropped his torch in the process, making the gloom around them all the more oppressive. Diarmid fumbled with his own torch, struggling against all hope and fear not to drop it, lest his nightmares fully come to pass. He burned his hands, but managed to get hold of the thing as he ran through twisting tunnels and ducked under stone overheads. The low moans turned into an evil growl as the creature gained on them. People were screaming – he couldn't tell who exactly. He might even have been screaming himself – he couldn't tell over the noise and his own soul rending terror.

All at once, the ground gave way beneath their party. Diarmid hit the level below with a sickening thud, and tasted blood in his mouth. Searing pain shot through his abdomen. He rolled onto his back, his mind spinning from the agonizing spasms in his solar plexus. The jagged hole above them was filled with angry spikes – and blood.

He looked over to his left to spy his torch, still blessedly lit. His eyes struggled to adjust to the sharp contrasts in light. It was then that he heard the noise.

At first he thought it was the moans from the creature before. That would have been preferable to the reality.

He reached around in the dark, blind, until he felt something warm and wet within his vicinity. Upon his hand making contact with the mass, he heard a sharp rasp inwards of pain and unimaginable suffering.

Diarmid rolled back over and struggled to his hands and knees, grabbing the torch as the ringing in his ears and head at last began to subside. He flashed the light of the torch in the direction of the thing he'd touch, and felt the bile rise in his throat. It was all he could do to choke it down and not vomit on the spot. Tuirean was laying next to him, deathly pale, groaning and rattling. His abdomen had been torn open in the fall. Intestines and other viscera throbbed with the rate of his ever slowing heart as blood poured from the gaping cavity. Diarmid panic pawed at the wound, paralyzed by indecision and unsure of what to do. In truth, there was nothing that he could do.

Tuirean let out a pained, rattling groan. And then he was gone.

Diarmid didn't have the time to allow himself to grieve. The screams of his other friends shocked him back to awareness. Rising to his feet and drawing his blade, he scanned the gloom in a vain attempt to make sense of the chaos erupting around him. Cian was closest to his position – screaming and beating back a monstrous figure in the shadows. Diarmid screamed and rushed forward, his torch light bringing their pursuers at last into horrible focus.

"Goblins!!" he and Cian screamed all at once. The creatures were shorter than regular men, hunched and ugly. Their green skin was such not due to any inherent hue, but due to the putrefaction their corrupted forms acquired over time. Goblins loathed the light, as the snarls and hisses of the creature before him confirmed. They were believed to be rejected beings from the lowest of Hells, so despicable and abhorrent to behold that even the demons of the realm loathed to be around them. And they were vicious.

The creature before him held a rusted halberd, angry and chipped from what could only have been decades of brutality and abuse. He was missing an eye – or more accurately, his rotten, shriveled eye hung loosely from it's socket, swinging with his movements. The creature screamed, it's putrid breath causing the bile to rise in Diarmid's chest, and then lunged at him with the weapon. Diarmid parried at the last moment, near losing his footing on a rock in the darkness. He was well used to holding his sword with two hands, but he dared not abandon the torch and lose the life saving light. The goblin lunged again, with Diarmid finding his footing and parrying once more, this time more effectively. Moving his sword into a high guard, he went on the offensice. Taking two rapid steps forward, he tricked the goblin into attempting to parry high and protect his other eye, before Diarmid shifted at the last possible moment to deliver a punishing strike at the goblin's left knee cap. The creature shrieked in agony, giving Cian time to rush in and deliver a strike of his own. In a moment, the goblin's head was on the ground and the encounter was over.

Cian and Diarmid stood back to back, each man doing his best to locate Devon and Geoff through the faint light of the torch and the maddening echoes of the sounds of battle off the cavernous walls.

"Down there!" Diarmid suddenly pointed with his torch. The two men broke into a run, racing down the newly illuminated tunnel fueled by the hope of rescuing their friends before it was too late.

Without even thinking, Diarmid joined the fray before assessing the situation. He had no choice. Two goblins had Devon pinned near a wall, and one more hit would have sent his friend to the hall's of his fathers without a doubt. Diarmid drove his sword through one goblin's back, the point of the blade exiting out of the creature's bloated belly. He withdrew his sword, now slick with blackened, cursed blood, and kicked his opponent down into the dirt before turning to face the next. The two circled each other, predator on prey with neither sure at just that moment who was which. At once, both struck out like cobras – Diarmid coming in with a high guard stab, and the goblin ostensibly rushing forward with a slash, until, too late, Diarmid realized it was a fake out. The goblin pivoted on his feet, and bifurcated Devon with his blade. Blood splashed in Diarmid's eyes, and he found himself fighting and screaming against a force that was pulling him back. He roared and kicked, attempting to break free from the force that bound him. A blow to the face brought him back to awareness. It was Cian, his sword as slick with black blood as Diarmid's own. His eyes darted around the room, at last adjusted to the gloom and mild light from the remaining torches.

It was then that he saw. Geoff was surrounded by goblins, and doing poorly. There was nothing Cian or Diarmid could do. Geoff had already been stabbed and slashed at numerous times, his skin pale and clammy from the obvious blood loss. It was hard to count though the chaos and darkness, but there must have been a minimum of fifty to seventy five goblins in the room with them. Diarmid winced through empathetic agony as he watched his friend disappear under the writhing mass of bodies and stabbing implements. When Geoff's screams at last went silent, the two friends turned and ran. To be sure, they were being followed. But the corpses of Devon, Geoff, and Tuirean were providing ample distraction to the hungry, degenerate pack of goblins at large.

The two friends ran and ran, Diarmid's lungs screaming at him their threats to give out even as he screamed all the louder. They ran until coming to an abrupt stop into a solid rock wall. Cian groaned and held his bleeding face even as Diarmid fell to the ground, his head ringing from the impact. He stood up as fast as he could, well aware that they weren't alone, and cognizant of the speed at which they needed to make their move lest these next few moments be their last.

"Which way?!" Cian exclaimed, pain and urgency evident in his voice, if not for a hint of terror. Diarmid pawed at the walls ineffectually. They were at a dead end. The only way out was back the way they came. There was no time for that, though.

A lumbering figure came into view through the gloom. Diarmid struggled to see through the shadows and gloom, but his heart sank cold as ice into the depths of his bowels. It was the goblin he ran through in his vain attempt to rescue Devon, holding in his vile viscera with one hand as it furiously swung its blade in the air with the other. Diarmid gripped his blade, his arms trembling from adrenaline and strain, even as it felt slick beneath his grip from blood that he could no longer be sure was entirely human, goblin, or even his own. Cian readied himself next to him, and then it happened.

The goblin roared and gripped his sword with both hands, no longer caring in its berserker rage if its insides fell onto the ground beneath him or not. Cian rushed in before Diarmid, and parried the blow.

"Run!!" he screamed at his friend.

Diarmid wasn't having it, "I'm not leaving you here!" as he rushed in with his own flurry of blows, landing several across the goblin's back. That only seemed to enrage it that much more. The goblin swung wildly at Diarmid, who back away just in time to avoid being disemboweled himself.

"Why won't you die?!" Diarmid shouted, crazed. The goblin merely laughed in response as it delivered another flurry, backing Diarmid into the wall. This was it, he thought.

Cian slashed at the creature's legs, getting it's attention. In response, it swung out once again, aiming higher this time, and Cian wasn't ready.

His head hit the ground in a sickening thud.

Diarmid sank to his knees in shock. It was over. All of his friends were dead, and now he was on the edge of his own demise.

He said a silent prayer to the old gods and the spirits of the barrow who surely were angered by not only his presence, but that of the corruption that loomed over him now, it's blade catching what little light remained. Diarmid shut his eyes, hoping beyond hope that even in light of his failures, he would still be welcomed into the halls of his fathers. Somehow, he doubted it.

That was at least, until he felt the ground beneath him begin to suddenly shift. He opened his eyes just in time to see the goblin's blade start to swing for his head just as the ground beneath him completely collapsed, sending him tumbling down into the blackness beneath him. He fell far further this time, and landed with a sharp crack on the ground. Staring up in the direction from which he fell, he could make out no indication of a light above or even the hole he came through. He sat up, searing pain shooting through his broken ribs, and prayed another prayer, thanking all the spirits that he was still alive.

Behind him, came a reptilian growl.

ROISIN

After two weeks of riding, at long last the visage of the capitol of Alderion came into view. She felt a sense of apprehension as she made her approach. She had survived this same journey once before, of course, but times had been very different then. Her mother had been older than she was now, and by then already an experienced shield maiden in her own right. Not to mention the fact that she had been a more experienced Lord of the realm – surely one more astute and aware of the political machinations of the Alderion High Court than she was.

Yet all the same, she couldn't deny a personal sense of excitement either. The actions of the High King that fateful day had stayed with her for a long time, and affected her far more deeply than she herself had realized up until the moment his letter arrived in her court. Gripping the reigns of her horse, a white stallion who had once belonged to her mother, and she imagined was all too glad to bear forth a true Snowstone Queen once again, she broke into a run and outpaced her retinue. Two hundred and fifty knights and men at arms had chosen to accompany her on this trip, and their party made up an impressive and imposing train. By no means was it an army, certainly not one capable of taking on the whole of Alderion's impressive Imperial City guard. But, it was an impressive show of force, greater than any Lord had dared to bring with them to a meeting with the High King in over three hundred years. Not even her late mother had been so bold.

Of course, had she not been in an emotion fuelled hurry, she may have taken more time to consider the repercussions of such an action. How her retinue would be received by the Imperial Court was entirely up to the High King's mood that day. But, what else could she do? Going to Alderion alone, or even with a small party of retainers, seemed like the height of foolishness to her. She had no doubt in her mind that the intentions of the High King were not positive. After all, Lusca lied far away from the city of Alderion. Assuming that shipping lanes stayed open, and produce kept flowing out from her wealthy realm, it would have been easy for the High King to forget about Lusca's existence apart from the religious complaints of some of the other nobles.

As she reached the city's gates, she brought her horse into a light trot and then at last to a stop.

"Halt!" shouted a city guardsman. He was a stout, portly man. Yet, something about him indicated to Roisin that crossing him was a poor idea. He held his halberd with pride, and his violet and red coloured uniform which marked him as a guardsman of the imperial household was immaculate in its presentation.

"Identify yourself!" he shouted at Roisin, still sitting astride her horse. Her retinue had now caught up to her.

"I am Roisin, Lady of Lusca," she responded, feeling it better to leave off the majority of her titles while in the city of Alderion, keeping to long established convention when among the Imperial Court.

The guardsman eyed the small force which had accompanied her.

"And why, my Lady, do you come with such a show of force?" he inquired.

"I have been summoned by His Imperial Highness, the High King. It have been a long ride from my realm. Would you have a

Lady travel the roads alone, and without protection?"

It was a clear attempt at manipulation, to be sure. But Roisin had never been above such things.

"I suppose not," the guardsman mused, his face still incredulous at the size of the force Roisin brought with her.

"I beg passage, as a Lord of a realm of Alderion, into the Imperial City," Roisin recited the same script her mother used once, so long ago now.

The guardsman gestured for her to wait a moment as he disappeared behind the city gates. This was unusual, as normally someone of Roisin's rank and stature would by convention be allowed passage into the city without question. Alas, the situation was far less than conventional, she supposed.

She and her retinue waited for some time. A cold wind blew in from the east. Normally Roisin would have found it somewhat uncomfortable and been glad for her black cloak, but with the degree to which her nerves were making her burn up, it felt refreshing. Soon, the guardsman came back.

"Lady Roisin of the Great and Noble Realm of Lusca, the Snowstone Mountains, and the Sunset Isles beyond the Sea. On behalf of High King Conn, son of Conchobar, Lord of the Ancient City of Alderion and it's Imperial Holdings besides, to whom you owe eternal fealty from the time of the Peace of the Dragons, I grant you passage into this city. On behalf of the High King, bring with you only peace and friendship, and leave some of the happiness you bring."

With the formalities over and done with, the gates to the city swung open and Roisin and her party began their advance.

The Imperial City of Alderion was a sight to behold. Towers stretched to the very limits of human ingenuity scraped the upper echelons of the sky, like spires capable of impaling the gods themselves. The streets were packed full to bursting with the hustle and bustle of imperial life. The train of arms and retainers that she had brought with her would not escape the notice of the citizenry, who stared at the party with a cautious, hushed amazement. Surely, high Lords and Ladies visited the city with regularity. But not in such force.

As if on cue, a squadron of Imperial Guardsmen approached her company. "Halt in the name of the High King!" the point man announced in an authoritative tone. The party ceased their advance.

The point man walked up to Roisin and gave the customary triune bow of a guardsman towards a Lore before completing his approach.

"His Imperial Lordship thanks you for your expeditious arrival to his summons," the man opened. Roisin grimaced, but allowed him to continue.

"He was not expecting you to bring such a large... party, but respects the need of a Lady of his Imperial Realms to stay safe upon the roads. The Mountain Clans are most troublesome, indeed."

The subtext couldn't have been clearer. The man went on,
"While His Lordship would love to host you personally within the confines of the Imperial Keep however, the size of the force you have brought with you makes that a prohibitive task, I'm afraid. But the Order of the Morning Star would be most pleased if your Ladyship and your part would grace their halls this evening. The stewards of the Order have already begun their preparations. You should find the accommodations most fitting for a Lady of

your stature. Please," the man gestured in the direction of the Order's keep, "Allow the Imperial Guard to escort you."

"I will gladly accept their hospitality," Roisin gave the customary slight bow of her head. The guardsman returned the gesture and the now far larger retinue made their way in the opposite direction of the Imperial Keep towards that of the Order. The outer edifice of the Order was almost as impressive as that of the Imperial Keep. At first glance, it would be difficult to tell which castle was larger, though Roisin half remembered from her education that it was in fact that of the Order.

The Master was already at the gates waiting to personally meet them. A flash of movement out of the corner of Roisin's eye temporarily distracted her from the formalities that were expected of her. A dove flew out of the upper rafters of the Order's keep. Almost as soon as it crossed the boundaries of the land allocated to the Order, three ravens flew out to meet it. The fight was no contest. A blood soaked white feather landed gently upon the head of Roisin's stallion.

In shock, she didn't respond right away when the Master greeted her using the customary terms. After giving her a moment, he loudly cleared his throat, snapping her back to attention. He reiterated:

"May the Light of the Morning Star shine upon you, my Lady. The gates of the Order are open to you and your party. We hope that you grace us with your presence for as long as it may please you."

"I and my party thank you, your Holiness," the word felt bitter in Roisin's mouth, but she had to keep up the pretense regardless. "We shall be sure to leave naught but happiness and fond memories in our wake."

They entered past the gates of the Order. Roisin dismounted her horse and it was immediately taken by a stable boy to the stables. The Master of the Order approached her, and after a customary bow, kissed Roisin's hand and offered his arm to escort her to her chambers. Were she a faithful member of the Church, her treatment would have been an honour. One glance towards the sullen faces of her accompanying Druids reminded her why it was anything but.

The Master showed her to her chambers, talking to her at length the entire time about the history of the Order, the grand magicians and priests it had produced over the years, and their role in the stability of the realm. At the least, it was interesting. And the Master seemed to be treating her with a modicum of respect, at least on a superficial level. He opened her chamber door for her, and showed her inside. The room was spacious and of a quality befitting a noble. One of the stewards, or perhaps a student, had already lit a fire for her in the fireplace and placed an assortment of wine, food, and reading material on the room's central table.

"I trust the accommodations are to your liking?" the Master inquired.

She nodded and planted a kiss on his cheek. "You are most kind."

"I shall leave you then," he stated. "Of course, you have free range of the Order and our grounds. I encourage you to visit our library, and of course, our chapel for daily prayer."

Alone now, Roisin took stock of her surroundings and left the few possessions she had on her person on the bed side table. Then, she felt the need to leave and visit the library as the Master had alluded to. The Order's keep was vast and meandering, but she didn't find it particularly hard to navigate – it was no Saelmere. The students and Clerics she passed all gave her the same passive deference. She wondered to herself what an education here was like for the children of Alderion's high nobles. No one in her direct family line had ever done so, primarily for religious reasons. The idea of there only being one god was too bitter a pill for most of those born and raised in Lusca to swallow.

She soon located the library and began to passively peruse the shelves. The attendants left her alone. It was probably for the best. While she knew what she was looking for, she didn't want to advertise her intentions for the tribunal any more than was strictly necessary.

"Do you need some assistance, my Lady?" a male voice from behind her said. She turned around to behold a handsome young man, around her age. He was dressed well in the finery befitting a noble, and stared at her with an expression of respect and perhaps a degree of admiration. His long white hair was tied back with a ribbon, and he overall looked neat, put together, and tidy.

Then her eyes fell upon the sigil on his surcoat – the raven black hawk of house Redwyn.

ELRIC

The woman jumped with surprise before looking him up and down.

"I'm sorry, my Lady," Elric said, "I didn't mean to frighten you."

The woman calmed down some, and graciously accepted Elric's apology. "It's no matter, perhaps you can, actually. I was looking for three tomes, but alas I'm unfamiliar with the standards of organization here. I'm searching for the compendium, obviously, but also the written versions of the sagas of Ildiachas, and the Grand Annals of Lusca and the Snowstone Tribes. Can you help me?"

Elric smiled at her, "A student of history, I see. Of course I can, my Lady. Follow me."

As though guided by the hand of the Morning Star himself, Elric located the books she was searching for with the upmost speed and efficiency. After their retrieval, he set the volumes down on a table nearby to a fire, and pulled the chair out to invite the lady to take a seat. She thanked him with grace and did so.

Even with his mission from the Master nagging him in the back of his mind, he couldn't help but feel inexplicably drawn to her. Her visage reminded him starkly of some of his own distant relations. She had to have some distant Redwyn blood to have hair that white and eyes that blue, and after all, his Grandfather was anxious for him to get married...

He shook off that trailing thought.

"If I may ask a question, my Lady, what is it that you require these books for?"

The woman wouldn't meet his eyes for a moment, before she responded "I'm to argue in a tribunal before the High King."

Elric could feel his own eyes brighten up then. Cautiously, he asked, "The one wherein the question of Luscan succession will at last be settled?"

The woman was silent for a moment, her eyes filled with distrust. "The very same. Unfortunately my Lord, I'm afraid I've already said far too much. Matters argued before such tribunals ought to be kept in confidence until they are decided, are they not?"

It was clear that Elric wasn't going to get more information out of her on the subject. "I suppose you're right. I apologize for prying, my Lady. Would you prefer I let you alone?"

The woman seemed to think for a moment. "I can read these in my own chambers. In fact, I would prefer to do so. But, if you don't mind my Lord, might I ask you a few questions of my own?"

Elric took a seat, "I'd be delighted to tell you whatever you'd like to know."

"You wear the black hawk," she gestured with caution, "should I presume then that you are a Redwyn?"

Embarrassed, Elric replied, "I've forgotten myself, my apologies. Yes, I am Elric, son Beric, Grandson of Lord Alaric. I'm pleased to make your acquaintance." He made a slight bow of his head and offered his hand. The woman took it and allowed him to kiss it.

"Charmed," she replied, "You may call me Roisin."
"A beautiful name, indeed,"
Roisin got straight to the point, "Tell me, my Lord, why your House believes itself to be the true heirs to Lusca?"

Elric breathed in deep, "That's a complicated question. Are you sure you have the time to listen to my answer?"

"Indulge me,"

"To put it simply, it comes down to matters of conviction. I don't presume to know your own leanings, my Lady, and I apologize for any offense I may give, but most of Alderion is in agreement that the Light of the Morning Star is the one true god of this world. Simply, Ildiachas represents a path of falsehood. It's an immature spirituality, focused I think far too much on the affairs of this world rather than the ultimate fate of the human soul in relation to its creator. To be blunt, I see it as emblematic of human willfulness."

Roisin was silent and pensive.

"I've offended you," Elric said.

"No, not particularly," Roisin replied with a sweet, forced smile. "Go on," she entreated.

"Well, if one were to accept that the Morning Star is the true Lord, then it stands to follow that nobility should follows His commandments. And the scriptures are clear – women are unfit to succeed a noble house."
"On what grounds?" Roisin interjected.

"It's a delicate situation," Elric grew anxious in his seat, "but the writings make it clear that the nobles are meant to act as his representatives. A woman can't represent the Morning Star, and it's said to bring calamity onto any house that rebels against it."

"Then why have the Banfion's lasted more than a thousand years? Was it not presumptuous of Elric the Redwyn to assume that his personal convictions trumped centuries of established, and stable practice? In general, they are known for being long lived and astute women. Far from suffering a great calamity, Lusca is one of the wealthiest realms in Alderion. Does their successes not stand in direct contradiction to your sacred scriptures?" she queried.

Elric sighed, "As I said, it's a complicated question. I don't pretend to be nearly educated enough in matters of religion to provide a satisfying rebuttal. That's for Priests and intellectuals to decide."

"If it's a realm you would lay claim to, then ought you not have a convincing justification for it?" Roisin asked, frustration clear in her voice.

Elric stared at Roisin for a long moment. "You follow the path of Ildiachas," he stated. It wasn't a question.

Roisin looked away, embarrassed by her lack of composure, "Yes," she affirmed.

"May your Gods smile on you warmly," Elric said in a genuine tone.

"Thank you,"

They were silent for a time. Elric didn't quite know how to continue their conversation, as much as he may have liked to.

"Shall I escort you back to your chambers, my Lady?" he asked.

She nodded. Ever the gentleman, Elric collected her books before offering her his arm, which she took with grace. Their walk back through the castle was mostly silent, with the occasional passing observation.

"I could," Elric started, "give you a tour of the grounds. If you like."

Roisin looked as though she were considering it for a moment before assenting. "Can we drop these books off first?"

"Of course,"

Once the menial business was over with, Elric set to work with his best attempts to woo the young woman on his arm with his knowledge of the castle, and the histories of the great Lords and Ladies who had studied within its walls. Roisin listened with what appeared to be plaintive interest, occasionally interjecting with a question or a word or two of affirmation to demonstrate that she was listening.

"Elric, my boy," a familiar voice called out from behind him. He froze, his veins turning to ice at his folly for having so quickly deviated from the task the Master had set before him. Turning around, Elric said to Roisin,

"Ah! Here is the Master of the Order. Have you been acquainted?"

"I and the Lady of Lusca have already been introduced, my son. But I commend you for taking it upon yourself to showcase the beauty of the Church's keep to our most distinguished guest."

"Of... Lusca?" Elric's eyes shot between the Master and Roisin.

"Yes," the Master said, "It grieved us greatly to hear of the passing of your mother, Lady Eafyn,"

"Thank you," Roisin bowed her head for a moment.

Realizing his lack of public decorum, Elric gave a swift bow before straightening his back, staring daggers at the Master.

"Have you showed her the gardens yet? There are some fine ferns all the way from the Snowstone Mountains. I think the Lady will be most interested in how we maintain a suitable climate for them."

"No, I've not," Elric gritted his teeth.

"I'll leave you to it then. But remember the task upon which I have set you."

"Of course," Elric offered himself back to Roisin, his mind still spinning with the implications of the revelation. "Shall we?"

To call the gardens illustrious would have been insulting. Their grandeur was so far beyond that of your average noble court that they could hardly be compared; they were akin to comparing the shack of a humble potter to the grand keep of a high lord of a realm. Per instruction, Elric brought Roisin right to the Snowstone ferns. There wasn't much of a trick to it. It was nothing more than a simple self maintaining frost spell that even a novice could cast. Still, he was sure that it must have been substantially more impressive than the cheap parlor tricks her Druids were capable of conjuring.

To his surprise, that wasn't the case.

"This is it?" she asked, her voice marred by ennui.
"What do you mean?"

With a knowing grin, Roisin flicked her wrist and conjured a flash of frost across the ferns.

"Your magic is not nearly as impressive as your Master made it out to be. Does he take me for some uneducated fool?"

"Since when did the Druids teach magic of any kind?" Elric exclaimed in shock. "Lusca hasn't produced a competent magician in 700 years!"

Roisin glared at him, and stepped in close. Her eyes blazed with fire. "Perhaps you ought to learn more about the realm you would usurp from under me. Is Aylemere full of as much ignorance as your reputation might portend?"

"What reputation?!" Elric roared.

Roisin smirked, "Exactly."

Having had enough of the humiliation, Elric murmured some words in Eldar before firing a bolt of purple flame at Roisin in a blind rage. She barely dodged the blast in time, the smell of singed hair filled the air around them, intermixing with the fragrance of exotic flowers. She stumbled over her gown and tried to collect herself before firing back a bolt of blue flame of her own.

"What is this madness?" a voice boomed from across the garden. The duelling pair paid it no mind and continued to exchange volleys. They might have gone on until one killed the other, were it not for the sound of a deafening crack.

Both youths' eyes snapped towards the darkened sky, now blacker than a moonless night. A firmament slowly formed across it, resembling a sickening silver vein with green undertones, as though the cosmos itself had taken on the same kind of corruption that claimed the limbs, and often the lives, of so many men injured on the battlefield. Their feud now utterly forgotten, all Elric could do was stare up at the events taking place. By now, people were pouring out of the doors and windows of the Order to catch a sight of the ongoing commotion. Somewhere, a woman was screaming. A crackling noise filled the air, and then

Nothing. Silence. Soundless bolts exited the crack and shot forth as far as the eye can see. And then as soon as it had occurred, it was over. The skies cleared back to as they were as though nothing had ever happened. Elric, Roisin, and the entire assembly stood for a moment in stunned silence, before the gardens and Order burst into a frenzy of activity. Two guardsmen seized Elric by the arm,

"Inside, now," they ordered. Seeming to not know what else to do, Roisin followed them without being told to herself. Hurriedly, the guards escorted the pair back to the library, at which time they were ordered to sit and await further instruction.

"What was that?" Roisin breathed, at long last.

"Nothing good, I imagine," Elric replied, unsure of what to do with himself. There was no way low level magic could have consequences that severe, he thought to himself. He reflected on the Eldar he had spoken, and wracked his brain for anything he might have done wrong. For the life of him, he couldn't come up with any mistakes. All the same, something was wrong, and his stomach sank with a sense for foreboding. Things were about to get a lot more complicated.

DIARMID

The growl was low and breathy, followed closely by the stench of fetid breath. All at once, Diarmid forgot the searing pain in his abdomen. He wanted to turn around and confront the beast that was behind him, yet at the same time his brain was screaming at him not to – as though if he were to ignore the noises behind him, they would cease to exist. It was infantile of course, he knew that. Refusal to acknowledge his problems had never been, and would never be, a means of solving them.

With great trepidation, he turned around to behold all his worst fears made manifest. The reptilian mass before him defied comprehension. He opened his mouth to scream but terror prevented any utterances from coming forth. The creature was truly awe inspiring. The cavern he found himself could have been measured in miles, but the dragon before him took up the whole of his field of vision. The beast bore a hue in a sickening inky black and its scales shone like stars in the sky. Green reptilian eyes glowed in the darkness, providing a surreal and otherworldly tinge to the already horrifying scene before him. The beast lumbered forward, its terrible claws crunching through the bedrock beneath it with every step. Diarmid felt the ground beneath him shake – it wasn't beyond the realm of possibility that yet more of the complex may collapse beneath his feet. He gripped his sword, the hilt still slick with blood.

"Stand away, monster!" he roared at the top of his lungs, pointing the tip of his blade at the maw of the creature. The dragon stared at him for a moment, before rearing back and opening its mouth. When he saw the wisps of flame in the back of its throat, he dove behind some rocks in scarce enough time to avoid his own annihilation. His legs and feet singed even through his leathers from the searing heat of the flame which served to light up the world around him brighter than even the most blinding of winter suns. Moss, chitin, and the remnants of old wood all came alight, and it was then that Diarmid beheld the true monstrosity before him.

He felt his mind coming apart at the seams. The dragons were gone – long dead and buried, slain by men of far greater stature and bravery than himself. But on some level, the same was said of goblins and the Sylven races and all other forms of magic that once made the world vibrant and filled with wonder when all was still young. Yet, unless he had been driven to the depths of madness, his eyes and burning flesh deceived him not. He had but one choice: to fight.

Summoning up the final reserves of his courage, he rushed the monster with his sword, darting beneath the creature's legs to drag his blade along the underside of its belly. It felt more like dragging his blade along granite than it did cutting through any sort of living flesh. The chips in his blade that weren't there previously were proof enough of that. The dragon whirled around, smacking Diarmid in the chest with the incredible strength it bore in its tail alone. The beast reared back on its hind legs, and through the gloom Diarmid watched pale, violet shadows rise from the earth beneath its feet. The wind had been knocked out of him. He could hardly breathe, let alone move as the phantoms from below coalesced into a ghostly beam that shot directly at his personage.

The pain was the most intense he had ever experienced in his life. Every moment brought with it a new and indescribable agony as his insides burned with the chill of a million tiny icicles. His eyesight blacked out for a brief moment, and he felt the bile rise in his throat from the visceral pain. He fell to the ground and vomited, his ears and head spinning. He wished for death to take him.

The sound of the dragon lumbering closer to him brought him back to some vestige of awareness. He gripped his sword and struggled against unreal pain to get to his feet. His vision was blurred. The sword held out in front of him, he prepared to make his last stand – lest no man say that at the end, Diarmid, son of Lukan, died a coward. The dragon prepared to make its strike with its mouth. Diarmid roared and brought his sword down upon the head of the fell beast. The blade shattered on impact, but not before taking a chunk of the dragon's flesh and a piece of its horns with it. The beast shrieked uncontrollably, black blood spurting forth from its wound like a waterfall. Diarmid scrambled, grabbing the pieces of flesh and horn along with the hilt of his broken sword before turning tail and running through the darkness once again.

Crazed, he ran through the gloom until he could run no further and then ran some more. He seemed to be ascending through the tunnels, but he had no means of knowing for sure. That was of course until he crashed through a wall made of earthen dirt. The cold, outdoor air reminded him at once of the demonic blast the dragon had hit him with and he found himself screaming in terror until his eyes at last registered that the light blighting them was not that of a conjuration brought forth from the deepest of hells, but that of the gentle, winter sunshine.

The world was quiet outside. Peaceful. There was not but the rustle of the leaves through barren branches, and the whoosh of light snow swept off snowdrifts by the mid-day wind. There were no goblins, or dragons, or devils to be found out here.

But his dead friends were no where to be found, either.

Brought low by that realization, Diarmid allowed icy tears to fall down his cheeks for not but a moment before rising and getting his bearings. There would be time to mourn. That time was not now. Clutching his evil parcel close, he began his long and agonizing walk back to the remnants of their camp.

Within a matter of hours, he reached the camp. The refuse of his former life, laid bare for him to see. How foolish they were to believe that they would only require a couple of hours, that anyone living would come back to this place, laughing and with a story to tell. Silent, he gathered what provisions he could before gently patting his mare. He mounted her, and with his broken sword, cut the bonds that held the horses of his friends – Tuirean, Devon, Geoff, Cian, all of them set free. After mouthing a wordless apology to each, he rode in the opposite direction, towards the castle at Saelmere.

It would be a journey of at least a week's time, enough to give Diarmid plenty of time to ruminate on just what he would say to Roisin upon his return. About his failure, about the deaths of his friends, about the problem festering below in their crypt...

The problem festering below.

Were not the Banfion's known, in times long past, for being prolific users of the magical arts? They weren't like the wizards of the Morning Star, to be sure. The magic of Lusca, the Snowstone Mountains, and the Sunset Isles was of an older sort, more primal and in tune with the elements that made up the world, both good and evil.

Evil.

He shook the thought out of his head and continued riding, blessing the bitter winds as they bit into any and all exposed flesh they could find on his person. He welcomed the pain, longed for it.

It reminded him both how alive he was, and how much he deserved to be dead.

During the night, he would do little more than erect a simple camp and a fire warm enough to prevent his death by exposure. The evil parcel had long since frozen solid, and he didn't care to keep it too close to his personage while he rested. It felt wrong to be near it, as though it amplified every negative feeling he had which had been well beyond considerable on their own. At night he slept but little, his dreams haunted by the rotting visages of all his dead friends, calling out to him from beyond the veil for him to give up the ghost and join them at last. After all, he knew it as well as they did, he ought to have died in that cavern, making it as much his own tomb as it was that of the ancient Banfions.

At long last and just as his resolve began to fail him at last, the silhouette of Saelmere came into his vision. Whereas before he found himself giddy with anticipation and excitement to simply behold that ancient keep to which he owed his allegiance, it fill him with an altogether different set of emotions to see it now. The stark black against the morning dawn now seemed menacing, as though perhaps the Redwyn's were right after all, and a woman ought not rule over such an ancient and prosperous land.

Where did that then leave Roisin?

He made his way to the main gate and kept riding even after the guard ordered him to cease his advances. The guards surrounded his mare and pulled their swords. He heard too the characteristic slide of an arrow being notched into a bow as the string pulled back. It didn't matter to him anymore.

"Let me pass or kill me here, but make your choice now. I've seen enough death and horror this week."

The glare he gave the guard was uncharacteristic for him, but something behind it caused the man to lose a fraction of his resolve. They conferred with one and other, until one at last had the wherewithal to ask, "Are you Diarmid, son of Lukan?"

Diarmid's eyes narrowed, "I am," he replied in a curt and impatient tone.

The guards looked at each other for yet another long moment before sheathing their weapons and dispersing. Diarmid rode into the castle courtyard before dismounting and directing the stable boy to take his mare. As his feet his the snow covered ground, clutching his parcel tight, he felt all those negative emotions come surging back, more powerful than they ever had before. Even watching all his friends die before his very eyes did not feel this dark.

Storming through the castle, his rage continued to boil until it reached the status of a raging inferno within his heart and soul. He burst into the main entrance hall, roaring in a rage that he didn't know the source of.

Roisin wasn't there. Few people were. Not even the little girl he'd spied on his first trip, or the non-descript brother. The hall was arrayed in the black banners of mourning, and the silver of a new coronation. Midir rose from his seat, traditionally to the right of that of the high Lady:

"Diarmid, my boy!" he greeted the young man with warmth, though his guard was clear. "I trust that you have completed your task?"

Diarmid gripped the parcel and his broken sword so tight he believed for a moment that the skin around his knuckles would most surely burst around the bone. His eye sight tunneled into the red hue of desire and homicidal rage. He threw the parcel and his sword at the feet of the Lord.

Confused, Midir rose from his seat and inspected the parcel. At once, he recoiled in abject horror at what he found – as though without a word spoken between the two men who knew exactly from what fell beast such an evil thing came from.

Beginning from his solar plexus and erupting forth with the strength of an ancient volcano, Diarmid screamed at the older man:

"What have you done?!"

To be continued.